You

Are My

Heart

and Other Stories

Jay Neugeboren

TWO DOLLAR RADIO
Books too loud to ignore.

For Eli and Jennifer

TWO DOLLAR RADIO is a family-run outfit founded in 2005 with the mission to reaffirm the cultural and artistic spirit of the publishing industry.

We aim to do this by presenting bold works of literary merit, each book, individually and collectively, providing a sonic progression that we believe to be too loud to ignore.

Author photograph by Eli Chaim Neugeboren.
Cover image: *"McCall's Magazine Cover, Woman Wearing Scarf,"* July 1938,
Nickolas Muray (American 1892-1965), George Eastman House Collection.

Stories in this collection were originally published, some in slightly different form, as follows: "You Are My Heart" in *Notre Dame Review*; "The Debt" in *The Gettysburg Review*; "State of Israel" (as "The Patient Will See You Now") in *Hadassah Magazine*; "The Turetzky Trio" in *TriQuarterly*; "Comfort" in *Black Clock*; "Make-A-Wish" in *Ploughshares*; "Here or There" in *Columbia*; "Overseas" in *Michigan Quarterly Review*.

Typeset in Garamond, the best font ever.

TWO DOLLAR RADIO
Books too loud to ignore.
www.TwoDollarRadio.com
twodollar@TwoDollarRadio.com

You

Are My

Heart

and Other Stories

Jay Neugeboren

You Are My Heart

It took three of us to move the sewer cover once we'd pried it up. Then the question was—who was going to go below and get the ball. Everyone looked at me, and I shrugged as if it to say: No big deal. Back then I was the kind of guy my friends would brag about because I'd take just about any dare—jumping onto the tracks in a subway station and waiting until the last second, a train bearing down on me, before vaulting back onto the platform, or, taking a running start, leaping from one rooftop to another—the gaps ran from five to ten feet—of four-, five-, and six-story apartment buildings.

This was 1953, in Brooklyn, and it was Olen Barksdale, my best friend that year, who volunteered to hold me upside down by the ankles. We were playing stickball in the P.S. 246 schoolyard on a cool Saturday afternoon in late October, and the sewer—a drain, really, that we used to mark third base—was one I'd been down before.

Olen and I were on the Erasmus basketball team together—he was a senior and I was a junior—and he'd been Honorable Mention All-City the year before when we'd made it to the quarterfinals of the city championships at Madison Square Garden. Most days after practice we'd take turns walking each other home, and a few nights a week, when our homework was done, we'd meet and take walks along Flatbush Avenue, usually winding up in a cafeteria, Bickford's or Garfield's, where we'd talk about everything—not just basketball, but personal stuff: about our families, and girls we liked, and why I did the crazy things I did, and, most of all, about how much we wanted to get away from our homes, and what we'd do with our lives someday after college when we were on our own in the world.

My dream, ever since I'd read Ayn Rand's *The Fountainhead*, was to become an architect. I was good at drawing and loved making model airplanes—I had a big collection of World War One and Two fighter planes—SPADs, Fokers, and Sopwith Camels; Messerschmitts, Flying Tigers, Spitfires, and Stukas— and not just the kind you carved from balsa wood, but the kind with rubber bands inside the fuselage, tail to propellor, that you wound up so that the planes would actually fly. You made the planes from what we called 'formers'—thin, round or box-like pieces of balsa in which you cut slots with razor blades so you could install toothpick-like stringers and struts that gave shape to the planes, and over which you pinned tissue-thin Jap paper you glued down and painted with dope. I also spent a lot of time drawing imaginary houses, complete with floor plans, and during the previous year I'd begun making models of some of them.

Olen's dream was to become the first person in his family to go to college, after which he intended to play pro basketball while attending medical school. That way, when he retired from the pros he'd already be a doctor, like Ernie Vandeweghe of the Knicks, and could afford a house like those most of the doctors we went to had, where your family lived on the top floors and you had your office on the ground floor, and where, most of the time, your wife was your nurse or assistant.

1953 was also the year I became the only white person sing- ing in the choir at Olen's church, The Barton African Method- ist Episcopal Church, and this happened not because of what he did when he held me upside down in the sewer—though that had something to do with it—or because of any dare, but because of how much I came to love the music, and—more— because I fell in love with Olen's sister Karen.

Despite all my bravado, Olen knew I was pretty scared when I did the things I was famous for. He was a very quiet guy— I think I was the only guy at school, black *or* white, he'd ever exchanged more than a few sentences with—so that when I crawled over the edge of the sewer, belly first, and one of the guys yelled out "Geronimo!" and I pushed off, I was surprised to hear Olen call down to me that the sweat was making him lose his grip, and that rats in the sewers had a real thing for Jewish noses. Did I know about this Jewish kid, naked and blindfolded and with a huge erection, who ran full blast into a brick wall? "Yeah," someone answered, giving the old line, "I heard he broke his nose."

The sewer was about nine feet deep, and Olen swung me back and forth like a pendulum so that my head was about three feet from the bottom and my hands were free to grab at things. The ball, a pink Spaldeen, was resting on a clump of rotting leaves, and as soon as I had it—the odors made my stomach pulse—I yelled at Olen to haul me up. Olen was all muscle, about six-foot-three and two hundred pounds, with wide shoulders and huge hands, and I was only five-seven and a hundred and thirty-five pounds soaking wet—and when he'd pulled me almost all the way out and I was bracing myself on the sides of the sewer to hoist myself up the rest of the way, he suddenly grabbed my left ankle with both hands and shoved me off again, letting me plunge back down to within a few feet of the bottom. I flailed away, my heart booming so loud I was sure the guys could hear it, but without letting go of the ball and without giving Olen the satisfaction of crying out.

On the way home, I gave him the silent treatment, and he knew that when I did, nothing could make me be the one to talk first, so finally he gave in and put his arm around me, telling me he didn't know what had gotten into him but that when he went to church the next morning he was going to ask the Lord for forgiveness. At first I thought he was kidding, and I almost said something about him asking God for a new brain while he was at it, but when I saw he was really feeling bad I didn't say anything, and a moment later he asked if Jews were allowed to go to church and would I want to go with him in the morning.

Sure, I said, and added that we weren't like the Catholic guys, who had to get permission if they wanted to come to synagogue for our Bar Mitzvahs. He told me he wasn't asking just because of what he'd done to me, but because it was going to be a special service where his sister Karen, who was my age, had a solo with the choir.

The next morning I got up before my parents did, put on a white shirt and a tie and, my good black dress shoes in my hands, tiptoed out of our apartment. Our street was quiet on Sunday mornings, with nobody going off to work or school, nobody yelling things down from apartment house windows, and only an occasional car going by. I sat on my stoop for a while after I put my shoes on, drinking in how peaceful things were—a rare moment for me because this was a period in my life when my parents were always checking up on me, my mother especially—wanting me to account for every minute of my life: where was I going, and who was I going with, and had I done my homework or brushed my teeth, and even wanting to know if I'd been having regular bowel movements. Both my parents worked, my father as a piece goods finisher in a dress factory (this was seasonal work, so he often spent long periods sitting around the apartment doing nothing, which drove my mother crazy), and my mother as a secretary for an insurance agent. I was an only child, and whenever the door to my room was closed she'd barge in without knocking and demand to know why I insisted on keeping the door closed and what I'd been doing during all the hours I was home alone.

Subtlety was never my parents' specialty, and though they never actually said anything *against* Olen, they'd say that they couldn't understand why, with all the choices of people I had to be friends with, I chose to spend so much time with a *shvartze*.

I had a pretty nasty temper in those days, and I'd yell at my parents that they were narrow-minded bigots who wanted to run my life for me. Were they going to choose my wife for me too some day? When my father was around and I said things like that, he'd whack me across the cheek, open-handed, yelling at me that I was an ingrate and a no-good, and the two of us would go at each other for a while. The angrier my father and I got, though, the calmer my mother became.

"Well, I always say the best way to judge a person's character is by the company he keeps," she would declare, adding that she certainly had nothing against Negroes, and that Olen seemed like a perfectly nice young man, although how could she tell since he never said anything besides hello, goodby, and thank you, and—who knows?—maybe the way my parents objected to him was part of the reason I was so determined to stick to our friendship.

Olen was a terrific ballplayer, but he wasn't the best player on our team that year. Our best player was a red-headed Irish kid named Johnny Lee. Johnny's father was a cop and his mother was a schoolteacher, and Johnny was not only first team All-City but, according to *The Sporting News*, a pre-season pick to make first team high school All-American. He was also an Honors student with dozens of colleges recruiting him, and the word was that he was going to go to an Ivy League school, probably Yale or Princeton.

He was almost as quiet as Olen—they were about the same size and build, with Johnny being leaner and an inch or so taller—and according to *The Brooklyn Eagle*, having the two of them work in tandem made us odds-on favorites to win the city championship. Although Johnny didn't have Olen's raw strength or open court one-on-one moves, he was a better rebounder, with a real nose for the ball, and he was a much better shooter. But then, there was probably no player in the city who was a better pure shooter than Johnny. In practice once, he hit eighteen straight jump shots from the right corner, and then followed with thirteen straight from the left corner before he missed. And he'd never leave the gym until he'd made twenty-five consecutive foul shots.

Most of the time Johnny would play in the middle, and Olen would roam along the baseline from one corner to the other, though they'd switch sometimes and Olen would move into the pivot. Even though Johnny often had to play against guys taller than he was, he had quick moves and such a soft touch, including a phenomenal fade-away jump shot, that eventually, in college, where he played at all five positions, sportswriters began calling him "The White O" after Oscar Robertson, who was probably the best player in the country during those years, and who, like Johnny, could play any position on the floor.

This was a time before college and pro basketball teams were dominated by black players—the first black player in the NBA, Chuck Cooper, didn't come into the league until the fall of 1949, more than two years *after* Jackie Robinson had joined the Brooklyn Dodgers—and it was a time before there were a lot of seven footers playing, so it wasn't unusual for guys Johnny's or Oscar's or Olen's size to play center. A few years before there had even been a player from the West Coast named Johnny O'Brien who was my height, or maybe an inch or two taller, who played in the pivot and had been an All-American.

It was also a time before sit-ins and freedom rides, before voter registration drives and bombed-out black churches received national headlines—before everything we know as the civil rights movement had come into being: before the Montgomery bus boycott and the Mississippi Freedom Democratic Party, before the Selma to Montgomery March and the March on Washington, before civil rights workers were murdered and governors stood in the doorways of schools to keep black children from going to classes with white children, and before riots destroyed black sections of cities like Los Angeles, Detroit, and Newark—before organizations like CORE, SNCC, SCLC, and the Black Panthers came into being, and before most of us had heard of people like Martin Luther King, Jr., Fannie Lou Hamer, Rosa Parks, Medgar Evers, Stokely Carmichael, and Malcolm X.

And even though it was also a time when what was called *de facto* segregation existed in New York City the way it did in most of the country, North *and* South, you wouldn't have known it from our neighborhood.

About a third of the students in my elementary school, kindergarten through eighth grade, were black, which was about the same percentage as Jews (Irish and Italians made up most of the other third), and virtually all the black kids, including Olen, lived in a three square block section—about a ten minute walk from my house—where their families owned their own homes.

Olen was the oldest of seven children, and he and Karen had come north from Georgia when he was in the fourth grade and Karen and I were in third grade. They came with their mother, grandmother, and brothers and sisters, but not with their father, and they moved into a two-story wood-frame house next to one owned by Olen's aunt and uncle—his mother's sister and her husband, who had five children, including the Tompkins twins, Rose and Marie, who were two years behind me. They also arrived with their Uncle Joshua, who pressed clothes in a dry cleaning store on Rogers Avenue, and it didn't occur to me until years later, after I'd moved away from Brooklyn and had a family of my own, that Joshua had not been a real uncle.

Starting in the fifth grade, Olen had a newspaper route in the mornings—he got up at five to deliver the papers—and from seventh grade on he worked after school, weekends, and summers delivering soda and seltzer, and he used to say that it was lifting the wooden cases and carrying them on his shoulders that had enabled him to build himself up so much.

Olen's mother, who worked as a cook in the lunchroom at P.S. 246—this was the elementary school Olen and his brothers and sisters went to with me—remembered that I'd had a reputation for being one of the smartest kids in the school, and about once a week she'd take me aside and make me promise to get Olen to study harder. Basketball was useful because it would get him into a college, but the main thing was for him to get his education. Before Olen was even fifteen months old, she told me, he could pick out any card you asked for from a deck, and where they came from in Georgia people used to gather around in their house to watch Olen do this. Nobody had ever seen a brighter boy baby, she said.

Olen's mother was usually in the kitchen cooking when I was there, and since a lot of what she made was fried in bacon grease and my family was kosher, the smells would drive me crazy, and when they did, Karen would delight in tempting me.

"Oh come on and have just a little taste," she'd tease, and she'd offer me a strip of bacon or a sausage patty or some fritters. "What do you think—that your God will strike you dead if you do?"

I'd resist at first, but then Olen, Karen, and some of the others would get on me, and while they fried up thick pieces of bread in the grease, or passed a strip of bacon under my nose, they'd roll their eyes and smack their lips with pleasure.

Mrs. Barksdale would tell her children to leave me be, but she'd laugh when she did. "Not eat bacon? Well, I can certainly see why you people are known for your suffering!" was one of her favorite lines, and it was usually the one that made me give in, and when I did—closing my eyes while Karen or Olen or one of their younger brothers or sisters put the food into my mouth—declaring that I was being force-fed against my will—they'd all hoot and holler in triumph.

When I got to Olen's house that Sunday morning in October, Karen was at the stove, and her hair, which was shoulder length and straight, was tied back in a lavender ribbon. The family was getting breakfast ready and Karen was working alongside her mother, both of them wearing aprons over their white dresses while they fried up sausage, bacon, cornbread, and flapjacks. "Let us pray," Uncle Joshua said after we were all seated, and everybody clasped their hands and looked down while Uncle Joshua gave thanks to Jesus for His loving kindness, for the food we were about to eat, for *all* our provisions, for our health and salvation, for the gift of song He had given to Karen, and for the young man of—his exact words—"the Mosaic persuasion" that He had given to us in loving friendship.

"That's you," Karen whispered quickly while everybody was saying "Amen," and she said it without looking up, her hands clasped in front of her.

Mrs. Barksdale and her mother left before we finished breakfast, and when we got to church they were standing on the steps with several other women, welcoming us and handing out programs. The church was made of whitewashed cinder blocks, with a big painted sign over the entrance, in red, white, and blue—"The Barton African Methodist Episcopal Church"— and above the sign, a plaster statue of Jesus on the cross, the statue bolted into what appeared to be a large porcelain bathtub that had been turned upright. The women were dressed in bright white dresses, wore turquoise-colored berets, sharply angled in front, that looked like the kind British commandoes used during World War Two, and had purple sashes across their chests, with patches that identified them as "Spirit-Led Women."

Inside the church other women, also dressed in white—eight or nine of them—were sitting in the back two rows, wearing blue capes and white nurse's caps. A group of older men, in black suits, ribbons on their lapels saying "Usher Corps," showed us to our seats, and none of the men or women treated me as if it was anything unusual for a white boy to be there.

I recognized a bunch of kids I knew from Erasmus—of the

five to six thousand students at Erasmus, only about a hundred were black, and just about all of them had gone to our elementary school—and, like Olen and his brothers and sisters, they were dressed in their Sunday best: the guys in shirts and ties—a few of them in suits—and the girls in fancy dresses. When one of them would look my way and smile, I'd smile back, but maybe because everyone knew how close Olen and I were, none of them acted surprised to see me there.

Olen didn't say much while we waited for the service to begin, and I didn't want to gape, so I kept my eyes on the program. "Shout to the Lord all the Earth! Let us sing Power and Majesty, Praise to the King!" the cover declared. "Nothing compares to the Promise I have in You."

What surprised me about the church was how *formal* everything was. Until I was Bar Mitzvahed, I'd gone to synagogue with my father every Saturday morning, and I still went with him a few times a month, and in our synagogue there were no programs or ushers or women in uniforms. People came and went whenever they wanted, stood up or sat down to chant the service in their own way and at their own pace no matter what else was going on, and people talked so much—some of the old men even snoring—that the rabbi would come to the front of the podium a few times during every service to demand quiet and to remind us that we were in the House of God.

The Order of Service at Olen and Karen's church was printed out, and the program also contained a Church Calendar for the week, a list of Daily Bible Readings, and a list of people who were Sick and Shut-In, with their addresses. When the service began—it was a "Special Harvest Service"—all the seats were filled, an usher and a Spirit-Led Woman stood at the end of each row of seats, and the room went dead silent.

Whenever Olen stood, I stood, and whenever he lowered his head in prayer, I did the same. Once people were paying attention to the Pastor, the Reverend Benjamin H. Kinnard, I relaxed, and when the congregation recited prayers—mostly Psalms from the Old Testament—I joined in, and when they stood and sang The Morning Hymn—"Jesus Hears Every Prayer"—I sang along with them.

As soon as we sat back down, an elderly woman in front of me turned around and smiled—"My, but you have a lovely voice, young man," she said—and Olen leaned into me, his eyes wide in astonishment—started to say something, then just shook his head sideways, and shrugged.

After that, the more Olen stared at me, the louder I sang. I didn't know the words to all the hymns, but I could latch onto the tunes fast and fake the words, and I found myself singing with gusto, so that when Visitors' Recognition came, and my name was called out, lots of people turned my way and applauded.

About halfway through the service, right after Tithes and Offerings (I followed Olen's lead and put fifty cents in the basket), Pastor Kinnard said that even as the harvest would be coming in, and not far down the road winter would be coming on, and even though dark times might be coming to any of us, still, with Jesus's love, and love in our hearts for Jesus, we could walk in the light, and when he said these words, Karen stepped forward from the choir. People in the congregation began talking out loud ("Walk in the light, oh yes, walk in the light," and things like that), and Pastor Kinnard said that Jesus had blessed us this Sunday with a young woman whose voice could make the angels weep, Mistress Karen Barksdale, who would now sing "Walk in the Light" for us.

"You watch this," Olen whispered just before Karen began to sing, and when she did—as soon as the first words left her mouth and rose into the air—it was all over for me. Her eyes were closed the way they were at breakfast when she was praying, and her voice was startling—clear, pure, strong—but it wasn't so much that I wondered how such a large voice could come from a girl her size—Karen was shorter than I was, and wirey—but that I wondered how she had ever known—how she had *first* known—that the voice she had was there inside her, and that it was hers.

The choir swayed from side to side, keeping the background beat by repeating the words "Walk-in-the-light," while, to one side of the choir, an elderly man played an upright piano, a boy of about ten or eleven played drums, and two of the Spirit-Led Women shook tambourines. People stood and waved hands back and forth, and when the music heated up some, and when Karen's voice soared above everybody's, singing out almost as if she were crying, but effortlessly—"*I want to be in love with Him!*"—I melted. I stood up then and sang along with everybody else, and when, warbling on the low notes, Karen's voice suddenly exploded into high ones and then shimmied back down, and when she sang out with all her might "*He's shining! He's shining!*" and the choir responded and they went back and forth with the words—"*He's shining! He's shining!*"—in what I would later learn was call-and-response, the place went wild—people stamping their feet and clapping their hands and turning in circles and singing their hearts out.

On the way home, I stayed close to Karen so I could tell her how incredible she was. Usually when I was around her, at school or in her home, she was easy with me: talking about her brothers and sisters or our teachers or homework or whatever was happening. But now, for the first time, she seemed shy, and it was only when Olen asked if she had heard me singing, that she acknowledged my presence.

"I heard you," she said, "and in my opinion, you have genuine potential." Then she looked right at me. "So I have a question for you, Mister Take-Any-Dare. Would you like to sing in the choir with us?"

For the next few months when I left my house on Sunday mornings, I took my gym bag with me, my good clothes packed inside as if I was going out to play ball with the guys—and two evenings a week, when I said I was going to meet Olen, I'd go to his house and then walk to church with Karen for choir practice. Our first time there, Karen introduced me to Mr. Pidgeon, the church's Minister of Music, and he sat down at the piano, had me repeat scales he played, and asked if I could read music. I said that I could—I'd had accordian lessons for a few years when I was younger—and he said that was good, and he gave me a folder with music in it. He said I would sing with the tenors, that he appreciated the quality of my voice—its "timbre"—and that (when he spoke the words, Karen showed nothing) I had "genuine potential."

We did a lot of familiar stuff like "The Lord's Prayer," "Ave Maria" (Karen and a girl named Louise Carr alternated on the solos for this), and "You'll Never Walk Alone," along with hymns and spirituals everybody knew like "Swing Low, Sweet Chariot," but the music I loved most was music I'd never heard before—pieces that seemed half-talked and half-sung and where, after you'd gotten through the basics, Mr. Pidgeon encouraged choir members to step forward and take solos if the spirit moved them to do so. Some of these songs were slow and sad and could start tears welling in my eyes, but the songs I looked forward to above all were the ones with a driving, insistent beat that became faster and faster, pounding away until you thought the church walls were going to bust open from trying to hold in the sound: "Don't Give Up" and "We Need Power" and "Packing Up, Getting Ready to Go"—songs that, except for the fact that they mentioned God or Jesus, you never would have known had anything to do with religion.

Mr. Pidgeon worked as a caretaker and groundskeeper for the Dutch Reformed Church on Flatbush Avenue that was across from Erasmus, and sometimes, when I saw him in the yard there, raking leaves or tending to gravestones, he would wave to me and I'd go into the yard and we'd talk for a while, mostly about my progress with the choir. "Control is the secret of beautiful song," he'd always say to me, the way he did to all of us at the start of choir practice, and he'd urge me to remember that passion without control was as useless as control without passion. If I remembered that, he told me, I could become a pretty good singer.

During the first few practices at Karen's church, I found myself in awe of the way other singers could make their voices do these intricate flips and wiggles that verged on screeches, and at how they could pull them back and turn them into soft liquid harmonies, or could move from minor to major and back again without the musical score telling them when to do it, and I was determined to be able to sing like them. I practiced hard and after a few sessions, and once I was warmed up, I found that I could get to the really high notes and could throw in harmonies that made the music richer and stranger—and I also found, with practice, that I could modulate my voice so that, almost instantaneously, I could get it to go from a full-throated howl to a soft whisper.

Until this time, I'd never thought of Karen in the way I thought of white girls I grew up with: as girls one might want to touch, hold hands with, or kiss. Now, though, especially after a practice or a service, I couldn't think of her in any other way. What was cockeyed was that when I was with her I felt incredibly comfortable and incredibly awkward at the same time. And when her Uncle Joshua or the Reverend Kinnard said "Let us pray," and she closed her eyes, lowered her head, and drew in a slow, deep breath, I felt something else entirely: a stillness inside me that was like the stillness I sensed in her. I would clasp my hands and lower my head too, but I wouldn't close my eyes because I loved looking sideways and watching her in profile, and when we were apart the rest of the week, and for years to come when I found myself in difficult times, I would often summon up a picture of how beautiful and peaceful she looked in these moments, and this would help me through.

The Friday night before Christmas vacation, we were scheduled to play James Madison at home. They had beaten us on their court in early December—our only defeat so far—but had lost one other game, so that if we beat them this time, we'd move into first place in our division and be on our way to getting an automatic first-round bye to the city championships.

This was my first season on the team, but because we were usually way ahead early into the second half, I was getting to play more than I'd expected to. I wasn't scoring much, but I was distributing the ball well and playing solid defense during the five or six minutes a game the coach called on me. Everybody knew how intense I was—in team scrimmages it was as if my life depended on every single play: if I didn't score, or steal the ball, or if the man I was guarding scored, I *died*!—but what Mr. Ordover, our coach, praised me for—and this, since I'd started going to choir practice, was new for me—was that for all my seemingly madman ways, once I was in the game I could focus and play under control so that I rarely made a turnover, or a mistake on defense.

We broke the game open early on when, during a six minute stretch, Johnny and Olen went on a tear and we outscored Madison 21 to 3. Johnny was having his best game of the year, outplaying the Madison center, Rudy LaRusso (who went on to have a long NBA career after being All-American at Dartmouth), and winding up with 32 points. Olen wasn't far behind, with 24, but best of all was that with a solid lead the coach put me in before halftime to give Jimmy Geller, our regular point guard, a rest, and when the guy guarding me dropped off to double-team Johnny or Olen, I fired away, hitting four straight shots from the top of the key.

We were a pretty happy crew that night, and in the man-by-man evaluation Mr. Ordover did after every game, he said that what was most important about my contribution wasn't the points I scored—I was third high scorer, with thirteen—but the intelligence with which I played. Intelligence, he declared, was what separated the very good ballplayers from the rest.

Most Friday nights after home games, we'd all get together in a back room at Garfield's Cafeteria, where, when the team walked in, the crowd would erupt in cheers. This week though, Jane Friedlander, who lived on Bedford Avenue near Midwood High School, a more middle-class section than ours, had asked me to spread the word that she'd gotten permission from her parents to have a victory party at her house.

As soon as I came out of the gym with Olen and the rest of the team, I spotted Karen—she was across the street with a group of her friends—and I didn't hesitate: I went up to her and told her that Olen and I were going to the party and asked if she wanted to come too. She didn't hesitate either, and after we got to Jane's house and took off our jackets and put down our gym bags, and while everybody stopped dancing and crowded around to tell us how great we were, she stayed next to me.

"So," she asked a minute or so after things had quieted down, "are you going to ask me to dance, or what?"

"Sure," I said, and I took her hand and we walked into the middle of the living room. I put my arm around her waist—the record that was playing was one of my favorites: Eddy Arnold singing "To Each His Own"—and I was so excited to feel her close to me—she let her cheek rest against mine the instant we started dancing—that it didn't even occur to me that people might think it unusual to see a white guy dancing with a black girl.

It was only later on in the evening, when the crowd had thinned out and I was standing around with some of the guys and going over plays from the game, that I realized Olen was gone, that Karen was the only black person left at the party, and that maybe people were noticing she was the only girl I'd danced with all night.

Usually at parties—or, the previous few years, when I was on our synagogue basketball team and we traveled to other synagogues for Saturday night games-and-dances—I danced with lots of different girls, and most times by the end of the evening I would choose one girl to walk home with and maybe get to make out. But this time I danced with Karen every time they played a slow dance, and each time we moved around the floor (she told me a few times how much she liked having me hum softly in her ear) we got closer and closer until, instead of letting her right hand rest in my left hand, she put both arms around my neck and I put both my arms around her waist.

A few minutes before midnight, Jane's mother came down the stairs and said that our parents were probably wondering where we were and that we should consider the next record the last dance. Jane put on Tony Bennett singing "Cold, Cold Heart," walked up to me and, in a voice that sounded just like her mother's, announced that I hadn't danced with her all night and that I now had the opportunity to correct this significant omission.

So I danced with Jane, and by the time the record ended, Karen was gone. I caught up to her within a few blocks, and when I asked if she was mad at me for not dancing the last dance with her, she hesitated, shook her head sideways, told me not to worry about it, and slipped her hand into mine. We held hands all the way home, and when we got to her house—all the lights except for the porch light were out—she tugged on my hand and led me along the side to the rear door. She let go of my hand then, leaned back against the door, and closed her eyes.

"You can kiss me if you want," she said.

Because my parents both worked in Manhattan, they didn't get home most evenings until after seven, which meant that all through January and early February, from the time I got home from basketball practice until my parents arrived, Karen and I were able to be alone in my apartment. We were careful, and would enter my building separately, and sometimes, if the coast wasn't clear, she'd go back to her house and we'd only get to be together for choir practice. Walking to and from church, though, we'd duck into doorways to kiss, and sometimes we'd find a car with its door unlocked and would climb in and make out in the backseat. A few times, too, Karen would wind her way through the backyards and alleys of my block, go down to our cellar, ring the kitchen bell—our apartment was on the fifth floor of a six-story building—and I would haul her up in the dumbwaiter.

The first few weeks we were together after Jane's party, we would neck until our lips were almost raw, and I couldn't believe how wonderful it was simply to kiss again and again and again—long, sweet, delicious kisses—and to try out all kinds of things neither of us had ever done before. By the second week of January, Karen was letting me touch her on the outside of her sweater, and a week or so later she let me unhook her brassiere and feel her breasts. After this, we took to lying together on my bed, naked from the waist up, and moving against each other, my leg between hers, or her legs around my waist, until I came. The first time this happened, I panicked and kept saying how sorry I was—"I'm sorry, I'm sorry, oh God, I'm really sorry"—and how this would never, ever happen again, but when I said this Karen just pulled me closer to her, stroked the back of my neck, and kissed me softly on the cheek.

"You are my heart," she said then, words she repeated the next few times we were together. When the same thing had happened about a dozen times, though, she started a new routine where whenever I said I was sorry, instead of pulling me to her, she would start giggling, after which I would insist that I was really, *really* sorry.

"Sure you are," she would say, then add: "But I'll bet it felt really, *really* good."

When she said this, I'd answer that it was certainly *possible* that it felt really, really good, and we'd burst into laughter, and grab and tickle each other until one of us had wrestled the other off the bed and onto the floor. Sometimes, too—one of our favorite things—we would stay there on the floor, face down, one of us on top of the other, pressing against each other as hard as we could for as long as we could.

When we were in Karen's home, or in church, we never held hands or touched, but the first time we went for a walk together when it wasn't to or from church—this was on a Saturday afternoon, in Prospect Park—she suddenly stopped and glared at me.

"Are you my brother, or what?" she asked.

"No," I said. "Of course not."

"Then why aren't you holding my hand?"

I took her hand, and after this whenever we were together, except for when we were on my block, or near her home, or in church—and even in the hallways at school between classes—we would hold hands or walk with our arms around each other.

Because we didn't dare make out in her home, and because our time in my apartment was limited to an hour or so a few afternoons a week, what happened was that we came to spend most of our time together talking. On weekends, and during late February and early March, when my father got laid off and was home all the time—we'd find luncheonettes on Flatbush Avenue, or on Empire Boulevard near the Botanic Gardens and Ebbets Field, and spend hours talking while we drank tea and hot chocolate, and ate toasted English muffins and French fries.

Although everyone at school knew we were going together, and some students and even a few guys on the team began giving us the cold shoulder—not returning our hellos, or crossing to the other side of the street if they saw us coming—and though doing what was considered forbidden back then (*West Side Story* didn't become a movie until a half-dozen years later) may have been part of what made our being together exciting, when we were apart and I thought of being with her again, I found myself looking forward to our *conversations*—to all the things I wanted to tell her—as much as I did to our physical closeness, because no matter how much we talked, when it was time for us to separate and return to our homes, I always felt we'd hardly even *begun* to talk.

Some of the time we talked about ordinary stuff: our teachers, or students we knew and which ones we thought were for real and which ones were phonies, or about the kinds of things Olen and I had always talked about—basketball, college, and what we wanted to do after college. We talked about our families too, but in a different way from how Olen and I had. With Olen, conversations were mostly about how we would do anything to get away and be on our own, and about what we'd do when we got there, but with Karen, I found myself talking more about what I *felt* about my family—about what it was like to be an only child with parents who made each other miserable and who took their misery out on me. I talked about how angry I got sometimes—totally out of control—and how this made me do some of the crazy things I did so that I could get my parents angry back at me and then have a justification for shouting at them or storming out of the house.

I knew my anger was probably a cover-up, I admitted, and that what really bothered me—why I got *so* angry—was because of how sad and lonely I felt a lot of the time. Nothing I ever did was enough for my parents—if I got a 98 in a course, why hadn't I gotten a hundred? If I cleaned up the kitchen and living room while they were at work, why hadn't I cleaned the bathroom too?—so that being an only child who was always being criticized made me end up feeling that some essential part of me was missing—as if, without having given me a brother or sister, my parents had somehow never finished making *me*.

Karen talked a lot about what it was like to be the oldest girl in a large family—to be put in the position of being responsible for her younger brothers and sisters, and to be blamed when they did things that upset her mother, her grandmother, or her

Uncle Joshua. She was determined to go to college, but whereas her mother and her Uncle Joshua were *counting* on Olen to go, the idea of Karen going to college was out of the question. Even though she'd always been a straight-A student, her mother had insisted she take a commercial course of studies so that when she graduated she could get a job as a secretary and help support the family.

My parents didn't fight me about *going* to college the way Karen's mother and her Uncle Joshua did, but I wanted—desperately—to get away to an *out-of-town* college, and, because my parents claimed they didn't have enough money to send me, they insisted I apply *only* to the city colleges—Brooklyn, Queens, or C.C.N.Y.—which had free tuition then. "With a brain like yours," my mother would argue, "why should you go somewhere where you'll be a little fish in a big pond, when you can live at home and be a big fish in a little pond?"

When I argued back that if I didn't win a scholarship, I'd work my way through with part-time and summer jobs, they'd become even more upset, my father yelling that you had to be a total idiot to pay for an education that wasn't as good as one you could get for free (and presenting as proof the fact that C.C.N.Y. had produced more Nobel prize winners than any college in the country, including Harvard), and my mother starting in with what it would be like for me to be a poor boy among rich boys at some Ivy League school where I'd have to work all the time, even on vacations, and how all she ever wanted in life was to spare me suffering.

So Karen and I talked about these things, and by acting out antic responses that even I, for all my anger and big mouth, didn't have the courage for—like telling my father the reason he wanted me to go to a place like Brooklyn College instead of a place like Swarthmore or Dartmouth was because it would show him up for the failure he was—we were able to laugh about our situations, and to console each other.

We also talked, at length, about our feelings and about how

wonderful it was to *feel* free to talk about our feelings. Sometimes, too, we fantasized about enrolling in an out-of-town college together—a small liberal arts school in upstate New York or New England, or a school that specialized in the arts like Oberlin or Antioch or Bard, where people would be more tolerant of an interracial couple—and how, if we had to, one of us would work at a job for four years and put the other through college, after which we'd switch, so that within eight years, when we'd still be in our early twenties, we'd both have college degrees and, married, we'd be able to start a family of our own. Mostly, though, we talked about how lucky we were to have discovered each other—and about how good it felt to be able to tell each other anything and everything and to feel understood in a way nobody else ever had or, we believed, ever would understand us. We also agreed that the biggest surprise for both of us was not having fallen in love after knowing each other for so many years, but that being in love had turned out to be—the word we came back to again and again—so *easy*.

The night before our quarterfinal game against Lafayette for the Brooklyn championship, Johnny Lee came down with the flu. He suited up and kept drinking liquids, but he wasn't himself and wound up playing less than fifteen minutes and only scoring seven points. Olen was a maniac under the boards and on defense, and, scoring thirty-three points, single-handedly kept us in the game, but by the time Jimmy Geller fouled out with four minutes left and the coach put me in, we were eleven points down. I played well enough, but the guy I was guarding, Stan Groll, their All-City ballplayer, pretty much did what he wanted with me, using up the clock by dribbling around near half-court like he played for the Harlem Globetrotters. I was able to steal the ball from him once, which, from the look in his eyes, he seemed to regard as an insult, but I also had to foul him three times to give us a chance to get the ball back, and he made all his foul shots. We lost by seventeen points.

With the basketball season over and my father back at work, Karen and I had more time alone in my apartment, where she tried to cheer me up by telling me obvious things—that, like Olen, I'd given it my best, that there was always next year, and that—believe it or not—she still loved me *even if* I wasn't on a city championship team. This helped some, but what really got me out of my doldrums was when one afternoon, as soon as we were in my room, instead of lying down on my bed, she started picking up and examining some of my model airplanes and looking through the windows of a few of the houses I'd made.

"Okay," she said. "Tell me how you make these things. I mean, how does a guy as restless as you are have the *patience*?"

So I started showing her how I put the planes together, and took a few old ones out of my closet (she remembered me bringing them into class in elementary school for show-and-tell, and flying some of them around the schoolyard at recess) to show her how much more detailed the newer ones were: pinheads on the propellor mounts to simulate bolts, blackened string next to the wheels to represent shock absorbers—and then I showed her sketches I'd been making for houses, and—I couldn't resist—the plans for a house I was designing for the two of us to live in some day.

The house was based on one by Frank Lloyd Wright, its main section cantilevered out over a waterfall, with enormous wraparound windows that would make you feel there was no separation between the interior of the house and the exterior. Karen liked the sketch, but what interested her more than the fact that I'd dreamt it up for the two of us, was how I was going to turn it into a model.

For the next week and a half, whenever we were in my room, we worked on the model, which, because it had huge windows that seemed to have no supports, was more complicated than any model I'd ever built before. I made the exteriors of most of my houses out of sheets of oaktag that came in different thicknesses, and I'd glue two pieces together, which made the finished product surprisingly strong and, unlike the kind of thin wood people usually made models from, had the advantage of never warping.

For the houses I'd made so far, I showed Karen, I began by drawing the main walls and roof sections on a single sheet of oaktag—the way, on the backs of cereal boxes, cowboy ranches, fire stations, or Army bases were made of one piece of cardboard that you cut out and folded along dotted lines—and with my razor blade and a steel straight-edge, I'd make half-cuts along the lines that showed where the walls and roof sections of the houses joined to each other. I'd prick the corners of windows and doors with a straight pin first so that the unneeded pieces fell out cleanly, after which I'd cut out pieces of celluloid a little larger than the window openings, and, with a phonograph needle held in a pin-chuck, I'd scribe in the sashes that separated the window panes, then tape the celluloid to the back side of the openings.

I kept most of my materials and tools (razor blades, nails and pins, files, compasses and protractors, scribers, small saws and hammers, rolls of adhesive tape, jars of poster paint, glue) in an old dentist's cabinet I'd gotten a few years before when our family dentist renovated his office. It had lots of compartments, including three flat slide-out drawers where I kept different size and color papers I'd been collecting for glueing to the outside walls—imitations of brick, stone, wood, and stucco—along with sheets of oaktag, Bristol Board, celluloid and—my favorite—a flexible glass called Perspex.

After Karen and I had laid out and put together the main section of the house (I decided to construct it in two parts, then to join the parts together), I cut out a large piece of Perspex, drilled holes in it for attaching it to floor and roof, and then, with a small Bunsen burner, began experimenting with warming it to different temperatures in order to bend it to the shape we wanted. The great thing about Perspex, which was almost as rigid as glass when it cooled down, was that it could be used for walls without needing any extra supports. The not-so-great thing about it was that it was almost impossible to find and maintain the right temperature for bending it.

About ten days after we'd been working together, on an afternoon when we were as close as we'd been to getting the Perspex to stay fixed (I'd cut out a curved piece of wood to use as a form around which to mold the glass), and when we were trying to set it in place on the model, we suddenly heard noise behind us—the front door opening and closing. A few seconds later my mother pushed the door to my bedroom open.

"What are *you* doing here?" she demanded.

"Helping Alan with a school project," Karen answered quickly.

"Of course you are," my mother said. "Of course you are." She shifted a bag of groceries from her right to left hand so she could wag a finger at Karen. "But let me tell you something, young lady—you don't fool me for a minute, do you hear me? You don't fool me for a minute, you *or* your famous brother."

After saying this, my mother did an about-face and left. I thought of apologizing for her—of telling Karen that my mother's bark was worse than her bite (which wasn't true), or of following her out of the room and *ordering* her to come back in and apologize to Karen, but I knew my mother would use anything I said to stir things up more, so I just stood there, and after a few seconds, Karen put down the tube of cement she'd been holding and reached for her coat, which was on my bed.

I pointed to the clock on top of my dresser. It was nearly seven-thirty.

"I guess we lost track of time," I offered.

"Yeah," she agreed, and then: "They say that's what happens when you're happy, right?"

She put on her coat, picked up her books, and walked to the

door. When she turned and looked back at me—her cheeks were flushed, a patchy rust-red—I wanted to rush to her and put my arms around her and tell her that everything would be all right, that I would love her forever no matter what my parents said or did, that we *would* go away to college together and have a home of our own someday, that if we stood by each other everything would work out…

"I'm sorry," was all I said though.

"Well, things could be worse," Karen said. "At least we weren't dry-humping on your bed, right? At least we still had our clothes on."

That night, after my father came home, my parents summoned me to the living room to tell me they'd heard rumors about me and Karen—"Love may be blind, but the neighbors ain't," my mother said, repeating one of her favorite sayings—but that they had talked things over and made a decision to let things run their course and not to interfere. They loved me very much, they insisted, and they knew, despite some of the things I did and the choices I made—my "eccentricities," they called them—that I hadn't *intended* to hurt them.

I told them I didn't need a sermon, and my father said that given how much time I was spending in church, I was probably right, and then my mother said we didn't need to be facetious at a time like this and, more important, that we shouldn't have secrets from one another: that it was time I learned something about them—something they should have told me long before this, and that it had to do with how once upon a time she had been in a situation not unlike the situation I was in now.

What amazed me was how calm my mother suddenly was. She was like a different mother than the one I'd grown up with, and when she told me the story, it was as if she'd been preparing to tell it to me since the day I was born.

Before she married my father, she said—this happened when

she was nineteen years old—she had become engaged to a Catholic boy named Tommy O'Connor, and when both sets of parents objected and made life hell for them, she and Tommy had borrowed a friend's car and driven down to Elkton, Maryland. Elkton was famous then for allowing marriages where, if you were under twenty-one you didn't need your parents' consent, and she and Tommy were married there.

When they returned to Brooklyn, they didn't have a place of their own—realistic planning was not their strong point, my mother noted—so they had returned, separately, to their parents' apartments, and their parents had taken each of them in. A few months later—without their ever having lived together—the marriage was annulled. Seven months later she married my father.

"It's all true—" my father said "—it's all true, every word of it," and he added that what they'd learned from this—given how their parents' opposition had only served to drive my mother and Tommy into each other's arms—was not to make the same mistake with me. So they'd decided that if I continued to date Karen, even though they wouldn't like it, neither would they oppose it.

By this time we were sitting at the kitchen table—my mother didn't want the brisket she'd prepared to get cold—and my father was making a speech I'd heard before, about how the point of it all was that he had married my mother, that they'd stayed married for twenty-three years, that they were still married, and that they would go to the grave married.

I asked my father if he wanted a medal for his achievements, and he called me a snot-nose who was still wet behind the ears. My mother seemed to snap out of it then, and talked to me the way she usually did.

"Here," she said, picking up the carving knife and leaning across the table, the knife pointed at me. "Why don't you just cut my heart out with this and get it over with now?"

My mother put the knife down, and my father, who was sitting between us, picked it up and placed it in front of me, after which he started yelling at my mother that it wouldn't help things for her to get so worked up and histrionic, and off they went again, arguing with each other about the best way to deal with me.

The big news around Erasmus—this happened less than a week later—was that Johnny Lee had chosen Yale, and would be going there on a full scholarship in the fall. By this time it was early April, when most seniors had heard from the colleges they'd applied to, and when it was warm enough for Karen and me to take long walks in the park together again. By this time, too, the park was the *only* place where we could be together by ourselves.

The reason for this was that on the night after my mother found Karen in the apartment with me, she had telephoned Karen's mother. The result was that I was no longer welcome in Karen's home—and when I went to choir practice, Mr. Pidgeon came up to me before rehearsal started and said that it was probably best if I didn't sing with the choir for a while.

Things were just as bad with Olen. Whenever I tried to talk with him, he became quiet and sullen the way he was with everyone else, and when I'd offer to go for a Coke and fries with him and ask if he wanted to get together over the weekend to play ball or do other stuff, he'd say he didn't have time to hang out with guys like me.

Karen said he was being the same with her, but that what was making him this way didn't have to do with her and me, but with what had happened between Olen and Mr. Ordover, and that what had happened was this: as soon as Olen learned about Johnny's decision to go to Yale, he'd gone straight in to see Mr. Ordover and had demanded to know what was going to happen to *him* next year. Despite the fact that Olen had good grades—a solid B—and had made first team All-Brooklyn and third team All-City—Mr. Ordover told him that the only coaches who'd talked with him about scholarships for Olen were from two all-Negro colleges in the South.

Olen had exploded, it seemed, and said he would rot in hell before he'd go to one of those places. That was all Karen knew. She didn't know what else Olen said, or what his plans were, because, as had always been the case with her brother, the more enraged he was, the quieter he became.

The next time I saw Olen, I tried to get him to talk about what had happened with him and Mr. Ordover, but all he did was to snap at me that if I was so interested in his future, why didn't *I* go in and talk with Mr. Ordover.

So I did. During my free period after lunch the next day, I found Mr. Ordover in his office and asked him if it was true—that Olen's only choices were two Negro colleges.

"It's true," Mr. Ordover said, "but what you have to realize is that when a college makes a commitment to a young athlete—the way Yale University has to Johnny—it has to be certain that the athlete will be capable, for his part, of honoring the commitment."

"So?" I said. "So why would that stop any college from wanting Olen to play for them? He's a good student—a lot smarter than people think—and an incredible ballplayer…"

Mr. Ordover praised me for being such a loyal friend, and then, switching subjects, started in about *my* prospects for the following year. He told me that unless some new player came along to beat me out, I would be his starting point guard, and also—excellent news he'd been saving for an appropriate time—that he'd already had inquiries about me from coaches with whom he had good working relationships. Not from places like Yale or Princeton, to be sure, but from some fine Division Two schools like Union, Muhlenberg, and Tufts, all of which were in the market for a smart point guard.

"But what about Olen?" I persisted. "What's *he* going to do next year?"

Mr. Ordover had spoken with Olen's guidance counselor, he replied, and learned that mistakenly counting on an offer of an athletic scholarship, Olen had, unfortunately, neglected to apply to any colleges in the traditional way. That was why Mr. Ordover had been speaking with coaches from several Negro schools where admissions standards were a bit more lax, and where arrangements for the coming fall could still be made.

"But he was counting on *you* to get him in somewhere," I protested. "The same as Johnny. Everybody knows that's how it works. The colleges contact you and you set up the rest the way you always have."

Mr. Ordover responded by saying that Johnny, for one, had applied to colleges the way everyone else had, that he thought Olen would do well in one of the schools he'd found for him, and—he rose from his chair and looked at his watch—that he had an appointment. Our conversation, he declared, was over.

"No it's not," I said. "You let him down, coach. He played his heart out for you for three years and you let him down."

Mr. Ordover said again that our conversation was over.

"No it's not," I repeated. "Because do you know what? If you don't get Olen into a regular college, then—" I searched for words "—then I won't be your point guard next year because I won't *be* on your team."

Mr. Ordover laughed. "You're not being very intelligent," he said. "Why forsake your chances because of your friend's obstinacy? That's just cutting off your nose to spite your face. The schools I can get Olen into, where he'll be with his own people, are good choices, and for Olen to allow his pride to destroy his future would be foolish beyond words."

"But you can *do* it," I said. "We all know it. If you want to, you can still get Olen into a place that isn't all-Negro. Coach Fisher got Sihugo Green into Duquense, didn't he? And Cal Ramsey's going to play for N.Y.U. next year, and Tony Jackson's going to St. John's, so how can you say the only place for Olen is with other Negroes?"

Mr. Ordover sighed. "Please," he said. "As a ballplayer, Olen is not in Green or Ramsay or Jackson's class—not by a long shot—and for you to think he is may indicate that you are less intelligent than I've been giving you credit for."

The bell went off for changing classes then and when it did, Mr. Ordover took me by the arm, led me to the door, opened it, and told me to get to my next class. What he wanted, he said, was to prevent me from saying anything I might regret later on. For his part, he was going to try to forget that our conversation had taken place because he didn't want my passion and aggressiveness—qualities that served me well on the court—to endanger my opportunities. I was, he said, echoing my father, still a young man who was wet behind the ears.

I knew I should have stopped myself then, but it was as if he was daring me to answer back, and when I was out of his office and in the large room where the secretaries worked and the other coaches hung out, I spoke the words that came to me.

"Intelligence?" I said. "*Intelligence?!* Let me tell you something, Mr. Ordover—in my opinion Olen has more intelligence in his little finger than you have in that crap between your ears you call a brain."

Word got around the school pretty fast about what had happened between me and Mr. Ordover, but it made no difference to Olen—whenever I saw him, he either evaded me or rejected my overtures—and it surely didn't help at home. As soon as my parents heard what happened, they demanded I give them a full and accurate accounting—which, in my righteous outrage at what had been done to Olen, I was happy to do—and then ordered me to send a letter of apology to Mr. Ordover. When I refused, they told me I was still the immature, selfish child I'd always been, and told me that since I was so free and independent, I could take my meals by myself from now on. And after that, they pretty much stopped talking to me.

Things got worse for Karen too. Although her mother's style may have been gentler than my mother's, the results were basically the same. Karen wasn't banished from the dinner table, but when she was there, everybody—including her brothers and sisters—ignored her. In addition, her mother and her Uncle Joshua took to blaming *her* for Olen's situation. If she was so smart, and cared so much about her brother, why hadn't she been more watchful—why hadn't she seen to it that he applied to colleges in a proper way? She knew how busy Olen was with basketball, with his weekend job, and with keeping up with his classes. What kind of secretary was she going to be some day if she couldn't even help her own brother with sending for applications, filling them out, and seeing that they were delivered on time? Worse still, they accused her of having neglected her own family in favor of—their words—an *unhealthy infatuation*.

Karen kept trying to get Olen to talk with her, and even went to his guidance counselor to find out if anything could be done about getting him into college for the fall, but the guidance counselor said that the only choices left for him were to go to one of the schools Mr. Ordover had found, get a job and apply again for entrance a year from September, or make a late application to one of the city colleges. But Olen had no interest in attending a school where he couldn't play ball, and because of the point-shaving scandals three years before, when star players at C.C.N.Y. had taken money to fix games (this after C.C.N.Y. had won both the N.C.A.A. *and* N.I.T. post-season tournaments), the city colleges had all dropped big-time intercollegiate basketball.

From this point on, whenever Karen and I were together, we spent pretty much all our time trading stories of how lousy things were for us at home. We still made out—kind of desperately—when we could find a secluded place in the park or an unlocked car, but although we didn't say it, it was as if we both began feeling doomed, and on walks or sitting next to each other in luncheonettes we'd go for long stretches without talking at all.

When I went down to the Holy Cross schoolyard on weekends for games of pick-up ball, the guys told me how brave and crazy they thought I was to have talked to Mr. Ordover the way I had. But when I suggested they join me—that if we all stuck together and we all refused to play, Mr. Ordover would have no choice *but* to make some calls and get Olen into a good school— I didn't get any takers.

Then, one Saturday morning in early May, for the first time since our season ended, Olen showed up at the schoolyard. He sat along the chainlink fence with the other guys, not saying much and nobody saying much to him, and when he got on the court to play against a team I was on—we'd won four in a row— he was at his best, scoring at will and jibing the guys on my team about how bad he was making them look. But then, his team up nine to two in a ten-baskets-wins game, when I was going in for an easy layup, he suddenly left his own man and instead of trying to block my shot, clotheslined me with a forearm to the chest that sent me skidding on the concrete, after which he just stood over me, smiling.

"What are you smiling about, you big ape?" I said when I got my wind back.

"I'm smiling at a guy who just doesn't have it," he said.

"Well it takes one to know one," I said back, and then, pain suddenly shooting through my arm, elbow to wrist—it was skinned raw—I felt tears rush to my eyes. I pressed my eyes closed, bit down on my lower lip, and when I opened my eyes, Olen was still standing there smiling.

"You're an idiot," I said. "Do you know that? You're nothing but a big stupid black idiot. Correct that: You're nothing a big stupid black *fucking* idiot."

The other guys crowded around, told us to go easy, and I saw a few of them get on either side of Olen, moving in to keep him from doing any more damage.

"Shut your mouth," Olen said. "You just shut your mouth."

"Who's gonna make me? *You?*" I stood up and stepped toward him so that the toes of my sneakers were right up against his. "Come on, big man—show us how smart and tough you are—how you always pick on guys your own size and your own intelligence, because you know what? The only thing smaller than your dick is your brain."

I saw fire flare briefly in his eyes, and then he just turned and walked out of the schoolyard. The guys came to me then, offering me their bandanas and handkerchiefs to wipe off the blood, and starting in praising me for how totally out of my mind I was to go at Olen the way I had.

"Fuck all of you too," I said, and left the schoolyard.

I caught up with Olen and stayed by his side for a few blocks, neither of us saying anything. Before we turned the corner to his street, though, he stopped and looked down at me.

"How's the arm?" he asked.

"Still attached," I said.

"But I mean it—I want you to just leave me be, okay?" he said. "I don't need you holding my hand or sucking around to do stuff for me. It only makes it worse, do you understand?"

"No," I said.

"Then fuck you," he said.

"You and what army?" I shot back.

"And don't always be such a wise-ass," he said, and he grabbed me by the arm, hard, opened his mouth—he seemed on the verge of saying more—but then let go and shook his head sideways, the anger suddenly washing out of him. "Forget it, okay? Just forget the whole thing and leave me be, you *and* my stupid sister, or next time—"

"Next time what—?"

He shrugged. "Maybe next time I drop you down the sewer

if I get the chance. Then you'll come out black as me, right? Black as the devil's ass at midnight!"

He laughed at what he'd said, but when I started to laugh with him, his face went hard again.

"You just leave me be, is all, do you hear?" he said again. "Do you? *Do* you? Because you don't know, see. You don't know anything. You just don't know."

Don't know what? I wanted to ask, but before I could say the words, he was gone.

I didn't see Karen that weekend—I telephoned her house a few times, but each time whoever answered told me she wasn't in—and on Sunday night, when I was feeling like shit because I was missing her so badly, my mother came into my room, knocking on the door before she did, which was a first, and sat down on my bed. It was killing her for us to be like strangers to each other, she said, and it was hard on my father too. What did I *want*? she asked. Could I just tell her what I wanted from them.

My answer was what it always was: for them to leave me alone.

But they'd been doing that, she said, and it hadn't made any difference. She said that my father believed that often you swallowed your pride and went against your own values, or you even lied—told white lies—to keep peace in the house. *Shalom habayis*, she said. That's what your father believes, and I do too. *Shalom habayis*.

I shrugged, and when my mother changed subjects, telling me she'd had a call from a Mrs. Merdinger, in Belle Harbor, I knew she was getting to her real reason for coming in to talk with me.

Did I remember a young woman I'd met at Temple Beth El named Marcia Merdinger? she asked. I answered that I remembered Marcia, that I'd met her at a dance the year before, after a game we'd played against her synagogue's team. My mother nodded and told me that Mrs. Merdinger had called without

Marcia's knowledge because there was a big dance at Marcia's high school—a junior prom—and that Marcia was thinking of inviting me, but that since Marcia hadn't heard from me in a long time, her mother was calling to say that it would be nice if I gave Marcia a call first.

I rolled my eyes, and told my mother to forget the whole thing, but my mother, sensing my weakness somehow—the truth was that Marcia had been one of the hottest girls I'd ever made out with—said that I didn't have to marry the girl, that all I had to do was call her and perhaps go to a dance with her. Where was the harm? My mother knew I was still seeing Karen, and if I didn't call Marcia, she would of course understand. That was my decision. But she *had* promised Mrs. Merdinger she would talk with me, so if I could let her know what I intended to do...

Meanwhile, I wasn't seeing much of Karen. Whenever I asked her about going for a walk, she said she had "obligations at home," and when, on Friday, I pointed out that a whole week had gone by without us spending any time alone together, and asked if she were avoiding me or if her mother and Uncle Joshua were putting pressure on her, she got angry.

We were standing in an alcove under the arch at the Bedford Avenue entrance to Erasmus—the school was modeled after a British university, built around a quadrangle with Gothic style architecture—and she kept her books between us, pressed to her chest like a shield.

"Am I avoiding you?" she asked, repeating my question. "Well, you might put it that way. But I'm not doing anything you're not doing to Olen."

I told her I didn't understand.

"You call yourself Olen's friend?" she said. "You call yourself his *friend*?"

"Sure," I said. "He's my *best* friend—"

"Then why aren't you spending time with him? This is when he needs you, and you're nowhere. This is when—"

"But he told me to leave him alone!" I protested. "He nearly chopped me in half last week at the schoolyard and then told me to go fuck myself and to never talk with him again—"

"And you *listened* to him?" Karen shoved her books against my chest, pushing me against the wall. "You *listened* to him?"

"But it's what he *said*," I said. "I tried—believe me—but he just kept telling me to leave him be, to—"

"Talk about stupid," Karen said. "I thought you were the big risk taker—the guy who never saw a dare he didn't like—"

"But this was *different*," I began. "He really meant it, and I just didn't know what else to do…"

"You could have talked with me," Karen said, as if to herself. She took a deep breath, and continued, without anger: "Olen's hurting bad—he's hurting real bad—the worst I've ever seen him, and he's been known to hunker down into some really foul moods. He won't open up to *anybody*. Even when my mother was so worried, she got Pastor Kinnard to come by the house the other night, it didn't do any good. So what's he gonna do? I mean, what's he gonna *do*? Answer me that if you're so smart. You're the only one could reach him, and now you just…"

I tried to put my arms around her, but she pushed me away.

"I counted on you," she said, "and you let me down. You let me down big-time."

"But what was I supposed to do when he said to leave him be—?"

"You were supposed to do *something*. You were supposed to use that famous daredevil imagination of yours. You were supposed to not take no for an answer." She took a deep breath, put her face close to mine, and spoke in a whisper, enunciating each word very clearly. "*You-were-supposed-to-be-his-friend.*"

Then she pushed by me, and walked away. I followed and stayed by her side all the way to her block, but no matter what I said—no matter how I pleaded for her to give me a chance to show her I *could* do better—she just kept telling me to leave her be, to stop following her, and to get on home. And when we got to her house, she told me we were finished and warned me not to telephone her or to *dare* to try to see her ever again.

By this time I'd had it, and I let go of the frustration that was boiling up inside me and told her that she was being as stupid as her brother, and to hell with both of them—that it was fine with me if we never saw each other again and if she ever came crawling back asking me to forgive her, it would be too late for her and me the way it was going to be too late for Olen and college.

Karen's grandmother came out on the porch then, along with two of Karen's little brothers, Edgar and Joel, and started yelling at me to leave her granddaughter alone or she'd call the police, and I told her to go ahead and call the police, and then for some reason I started in singing as loud as I could the first song that came into my head—"Oh Happy Day"—and asking her and Karen to join in with me, and when her grandmother went back inside and I kept singing, Karen told me I was truly nuts and that her grandmother meant what she said and that I'd better get out of there.

I thanked Karen for being concerned for my safety, and walked down the street—the Tompkins twins came out onto their porch and made circles at the sides of their heads with their index fingers, which they then pointed at me to show that they agreed with Karen about me being nuts—and I just waved to them and kept singing at the top of my lungs—"*Oh happy day… Oh happy day…*"—but with, I hoped Karen would notice, the best voice control I'd ever had.

By the time I got home I was feeling pretty low, and I telephoned Karen at least a half-dozen times before supper, but each time when I said "Is Karen there?" the person on the other end hung up on me. I walked from room to room of my apartment, then picked up the model of the house we'd been working on and in a sudden fit of frustration almost threw it against the wall, but instead I set it down gently on my desk and caressed it as if it were a puppy, and spoke to it, telling it that everything was going to be all right. All I really wanted was to erase everything that had been happening, and for things to be okay between me and Karen the way they'd been before I'd shot my mouth off at Mr. Ordover. All I really wanted, I knew, was for somebody to tell *me* everything would be all right—to talk to *me* with some tenderness.

I lay down on my bed then and, imagining Karen was there with me, I closed my eyes and unzipped my fly. The next thing I knew, the phone rang but I was in such a deep sleep that at first I didn't know where I was or what time it was. I stumbled into the foyer, where our telephone was.

"Hi. This is Marcia, from Belle Harbor," the voice said. "Your old flame."

I said something back about being glad to hear from her, and she said she was only calling because she wanted me to know that she hadn't put *her* mother up to calling *my* mother. In fact, she had no idea how her mother even got my phone number.

"And I'm not calling to get you to go to the prom with me," she added. "I just wanted you to know that I didn't put my mother up to calling. *God!*"

"I figured," I said. "I mean, I figured you had nothing to do with it."

"And also, as long as we're talking, that I followed your team this year. I saw a lot of your box scores."

"You *did*?!"

"Sure. Some girls like saxophone players, but—shh: don't tell anybody—I've always had a thing for basketball players."

"Well, we lost the big one—"

"Lose the game, win the girl—" she said quickly.

"Which one?"

"The girl of your dreams."

"Sure," I said.

"Only listen," she said. "I'm probably embarassing you—which is definitely my intention—but I really did want you to know what happened, and also that if you invite me to the prom, I'll go with you."

"Don't do me any favors," I said back, and when I did she laughed.

"Really, though," she said. "I was just pulling your chain. You don't have to go with me. I mean, it's no big deal. Only—"

"Only what—?"

"I heard you were seeing somebody—keeping company, as my mother likes to put it."

"We broke up," I said. "I mean, we *just* broke up—"

"Oh Jesus," she said. "Sorry and double-sorry."

Then, after she apologized some more for giving me such a hard time, she told me the story of what happened when she'd broken up with *her* boyfriend at the end of the summer—he wasn't black, but he wasn't Jewish either—and about how her parents had been on her case and how devastated she'd been, and I said I didn't think that part of it—being devastated—had hit me yet. When I told her that my best *guy*-friend wasn't talking to me either—I didn't tell her he was Karen's brother—and that it felt good to talk to *someone*—her voice got softer and she said I could call her anytime I wanted to talk. She knew what I was going through, she said, and she knew it helped to talk with somebody who'd been there too.

We stayed on the phone for a long time, talking a lot about how our parents had bugged us, and we wound up deciding that the two of us could probably become Platonic friends—maybe even introduce each other to guys and girls we knew and double date some day, but that until then, where would the harm be if we called each other sometimes just to talk, or if I came out on Saturday night and we went to the prom together? If nothing else, it would make things easier for us at home with our parents so that we'd be freer to do what we wanted to do *outside* our homes. I asked about arrangements, and she said not to worry about a tux—it wasn't formal—and that she'd call me back later in the evening with details.

Instead of Marcia calling back, though, her mother called my mother to say that given the bus ride out to Belle Harbor, and given the fact that the dance might end late, I was welcome to stay over on Saturday night in their guest room.

So I went to the prom, and Marcia and I danced close all night, with her blowing in my ear sometimes and telling me she remembered what a great dancer I was and that if she remembered correctly, I was a pretty good kisser too. Mostly, though, she seemed happy just to be there, and to show me off to her friends—some of whom had seen me play in Madison Square Garden, and remembered when I'd come out to Belle Harbor before.

After the dance, we went to one of her friends' houses—all the kids from her crowd lived in private homes with garages, yards, and finished basements—and some of her friends passed around flasks of whiskey. There was a lot of necking and slow dancing, with the lights out except for a few candles, and some of the couples disappeared into other rooms. Marcia could tell I wasn't in the mood for much, and when she asked if I was mooning over my girlfriend, I admitted that I was, so after a while, and without making out, she suggested we go back to her house.

Her parents were still up when we got there, and we talked with them about the prom, and about which of Marcia's friends had been there with which guys, and then Marcia said that we were both pretty tired, and her parents said how nice it was to see me again and told me they would see me at breakfast. Marcia showed me to the guest room in the basement, took some stuffed animals and extra pillows off the bed, told me she'd had a lovely time, thanked me for coming, especially given what I'd been going through, gave me a quick kiss on the cheek, and left.

In the middle of the night, though—the clock-radio on the night table said it was 3:22—she woke me, lifted the covers, and got into the bed next to me.

"The bad news is that I couldn't sleep," she said. "But that's the good news too, along with the fact that my parents *are* fast asleep. I hope you don't mind."

All she was wearing was a thin nightgown, and she started caressing me, then giving me these little bites up and down my body that drove me crazy, all the while asking, "Do you like that…? Do you like *that*…? Do you *like* that…?" and telling me that anytime I wanted her to stop all I had to do was say so.

On Tuesday of the next week, Karen waited for me after school and asked me to go for a walk with her. We stayed silent all along Flatbush Avenue until we got to the park, and then she told me she'd heard that I'd gone to a dance in Belle Harbor and asked if I wanted to tell her about it.

I shrugged, and asked what was there to tell, given that she had said we were finished with each other.

"So that means I *made* you go to the dance with another girl, right?"

"No," I said. "But it—the dance—didn't mean anything. I mean, my mother was after me—the girl's mother called my mother and—"

"So you were *forced* to go by events beyond your control, is that it?"

I told her that I went to the dance because I wanted to—that she and I were both free to do what we wanted, weren't we? Were we engaged? Were we even going steady anymore?

"I trusted you," she said. "I loved you and I trusted you and in one week, you just…"

She stopped talking, and I could see she was working hard to keep from crying.

"You really stink, do you know that?" she said then. "But do you know the worst part? The worst part is that I still care for you more than is good for me, and I probably always will, so this is what I want to say: If you're willing to try again—no matter our parents, or Olen, or our skin, or whatever—I'm willing."

"So?" I asked.

"So?" she exclaimed. "*So?!* So *are* you? Do *you* want to try again?"

"Look," I began. "I really do care for you, only—"

"Only you just answered my question," she said. "Lord help you. You're breaking my heart, but do you know what? At least I've got a heart to break."

And that was the last time we ever spoke.

Olen didn't go to college the following fall, and as far as I know he never went. But Karen did. In September, 1955, when I went off to college—Hamilton College, in upstate New York, where, even though I stuck to my word and didn't play for Mr. Ordover during my senior year at Erasmus, I was able to make the Hamilton team and became its starting point guard my junior year—Karen took a job as a secretary for a toy manufacturer in downtown Brooklyn.

Whenever I came home on school vacations, and after college too, I'd ask around about her, and what I learned was that after a year or two as a secretary, she'd started going to Brooklyn College at night and during the summers, after which she did the same thing at Brooklyn Law School.

Sometime in the early sixties, I was told, her family moved out of Brooklyn, but nobody could tell me exactly where they'd gone, and none of the guys knew what happened to Olen either. The year after he graduated, he'd worked for a while in the stock room at the new Macy's department store on Flatbush Avenue, and after that there were rumors about him getting a try-out with the Harlem Globetrotters, or with the team of mostly white guys the Globetrotters toured with, but nobody knew for sure.

When, in the summer of 1964, I took time out of school—I was in my last year at the Yale School of Architecture—to work down South helping to register voters, I found myself imagining—hoping—that Karen would be assigned to the same team I was on, that we'd meet and realize we still loved each other and that there was no force on earth strong enough to keep us from being together.

But we didn't meet down there, and the following summer—in June, 1965—I married Allison Plaut, a Jewish girl from Cleveland I fell in love with when she was a Yale junior and I was working as an apprentice architect for a company in the New Haven shipyards. After living in the New Haven area for eight years, I accepted a position in the design department of an international ship-building company near Baton Rouge, Louisiana, and Allison and I moved down there, where we raised our family—a girl and two boys—and where Allison worked first as an elementary school teacher, and later on as a professor in the School of Education at L.S.U., and where, once a year, with our children, and then by ourselves after our children went off to college, we'd drive down to New Orleans for Jazz Fest, where, no matter what other musicians were performing, I'd wind up spending all my time in the gospel tent, sometimes singing along to songs I remembered.

Here or There

When Peter Simmons had visited South Africa the previous summer, he had become concerned about several HIV-infected patients in Tugela Ferry who had died from a strain of tuberculosis that had proven resistant to all known drugs. Upon his return to the States, Peter, who was Professor of Medicine and Director of AIDS Programs at Johns Hopkins Medical School, had alerted the CDC to his discovery, and it turned out that the strain of tuberculosis, its identity obtained through molecular fingerprinting, had been known to the CDC since 1995. What they needed now, they told Peter, was a live culture of the bacteria in order to determine if other strains like it existed.

Their attempts to acquire samples of the organism itself, however, had been thwarted by the South African government, which would not allow representatives of the CDC to enter the country. Perhaps, they suggested, when Peter was next in Tugela Ferry, he could obtain a culture and bring it back with him. And perhaps, Peter thought, he could persuade his daughter, Jennifer, who would arouse considerably less suspicion than he would, to accompany him to South Africa and to transport the sample. Perhaps, too, the assignment—its adventure—would distract her from her situation.

The best time to plant a tree is twenty years ago. The second best time is now. The African proverb had been with Peter intermittently thoughout the day, the words softly and insistently repeating themselves, and they were with him again now while he sat at a café with Jennifer, an electric brazier beside their table giving off enough heat on this early December day to enable them to sit outside.

Jennifer pointed to the large parking lot that took up most of the center of Saint Rémy—she had been staying in the town, on leave from her job, for more than two weeks now—and said that several mornings a week, the parking lot, along with many of the side streets that radiated from it, was transformed into a market.

"I could be happy living here," she said.

"Who wouldn't?" Peter said.

"It's a real *village*—a place where you can shop every day for the things you need for that day, and where you know the shopkeepers, where their children are friends with your children—"

"You don't *have* any children."

"It has all the perks of a larger city too," Jennifer continued. "Museums, music festivals, art galleries. Lots of writers and artists live here—it's not far from major cities, and from the sea—even from the Alps, if you travel inland a bit—"

"You're in a good mood, aren't you?"

"What could be bad?" Jennifer said. "I'm far from my phone, my computer, and my law office. I'm in a beautiful village in the south of France where—lucky me—I'm having a fashionable late-afternoon drink with my father."

"And you're pregnant."

"Oh *that*!" Jennifer said, and waved the subject away.

"You didn't answer my question."

"You didn't *ask* a question."

Peter leaned across the table. "Jennifer," he said.

"*Dad*," she said, leaning toward him in the way he was leaning toward her.

"Look. We've *got* to talk about what you're going to do. I have no intention of telling you *what* to do, of course, but—"

"But nothing, okay?" Jennifer said. "So how about, instead

of you telling me the-choices-are-mine-but-you-just-want-to-make-sure-I-understand-the-consequences—you tell me what you think. How about—even better—you tell me *what to do*! It would be a relief, believe me, to have somebody just take over."

"I need more data," Peter said. "What week are you in? Have you had an ultrasound yet? Do you love the guy? Does he know?"

"Last question first. He doesn't know *and* I don't love him. I surely had the *hots* for him, but I've concluded that if I never saw him again, it wouldn't be too soon. I don't *miss* him. Plus, he'd make a *lousy* father—the kind of guy who'd say, 'You deserve to have your career, dear, so I'll play Mister Mom for our kids'— and then I'd arrive home to find him zoned out in front of the TV—yes, he's a pot-head too—the house a wreck, the baby ass deep in poop and puke, and—"

"Do you want the child?"

"Maybe."

"Not good enough," Peter said.

Jennifer looked away. She lifted her glass of wine, then set it back on the table. "I probably shouldn't be having any alcohol," she said. "Why didn't you stop me?"

"You're a big girl," Peter said. "And one drink won't cause birth defects. All things in moderation."

"Including moderation, right?" Jennifer sighed. "But look— I know you think it would be good for me to go with you to South Africa instead of staying here and worrying my decision to death, not to mention causing my loving parents unnecessary anguish, but—" She stopped, waved her hand in front of his eyes. "Dad? *Dad?!* Are you *listening* to me?"

"Of course. You think I think it would be good for you to come with me to South Africa and that—"

"*No!*" Jennifer slammed the table with the flat of her hand. "No. You can parrot my words back well enough, but you're staring at that woman over there. It's rude."

Peter *had* noticed a woman sitting a few tables away: an attractive, dark-haired woman, her shoulder-length hair parted to one side—in her mid-forties, he guessed—who was drinking coffee and reading a newspaper.

"I thought she might be someone I knew," Peter said. "She looked familiar."

"They *all* look familiar," Jennifer said, and, nearly knocking over her glass of wine, leaned forward and slammed her hand on the table again. "I hate it when men do that—I absolutely hate it when they pretend to be listening while ogling another woman, and when a guy does it to me what I want to do is to pull an ice pick out of my handbag and jab it in one of his eyes. If we could do that to every man who thinks he has the right to stare at us that way, and if—"

"Stop it. People are staring at *you*."

Jennifer sat back. "Okay," she said. "I'm done for now. And yes, I did come here because of Van Gogh—because he spent the last year of his life here, before he killed himself—but rest assured I am not necessarily suicidal. I just like the peace and quiet—the beauty of the landscape that inspired him even while he was locked up and out of his mind—and I like being far from everything and everyone I know, and it was probably a mistake for you to visit me. Correct that. It was probably a mistake for me to say yes when you said you wanted to stop by on your way to do more of God's work."

Jennifer forced a smile, then leaned back. "I'll be fine in a few years," she said.

"I'm counting on it," Peter said. Then: "Any morning sickness?"

"No."

"Been to a doctor?"

"Sure."

"Okay," he said. "What I think, then, is that you should have the child."

Jennifer grinned. "Thank God," she said. "I was hoping you'd say that. So okay: here or there?"

"There."

"Do I tell the father?"

"Not necessarily. If he finds out, there could be legal complications. We need to know more first—to inform ourselves."

"What if I don't do what you say—what if I don't have the child?"

"Then you don't."

Jennifer cocked her head to the side. "You *are* a good man, you know," she said. "Mom always said so, even when she was pissed at you. Maybe not the best dad in the world—you were *away* so damned much, and playing around, and—"

"Now wait a minute—" Peter began.

"Oh Dad, it doesn't matter. I think it may have mattered to Mom in the beginning—she never said anything to me, but—" Jennifer stopped. "When I think about marriage—about finding a guy I'd want to have children with, and when I think about my age—past thirty—*wow!*—I mean, the idea of making love to one man and one man only for the next twenty or thirty years, it seems utterly ridiculous. I don't get how people do it."

"Maybe they don't."

"But then there's all the secrecy and lying and sneaking around and hurt feelings. It all seems so stupid."

"What's the alternative?"

Jennifer shrugged. "Living in France?"

Peter laughed.

"I've been angry with you—sure—but not for that," Jennifer said. "I mean, you were working so damned hard all those years, going out to save lives every day, and when—"

"*Save* lives? Not at all. Mostly they *died*. For every life I saved—prolonged, at best—at least a hundred died. Look. At last count in Tugela Ferry alone, fifty-two HIV-infected people have died from the strain of TB I was telling you about. And in just the short while we've been sitting here and talking, thousands of *children* have died of AIDS. More than eight thousand people *a day* are dying of AIDS—"

"I don't *need* to hear this now, okay?" Jennifer said, covering her ears with both hands. "You don't get it, Dad. You just don't get it, do you? You're always so fucking righteous and *correct. That's* the big problem. I mean, are you *ever* wrong? Have you ever done *anything* wrong?"

"Evidently—to judge by your anger—I've done lots wrong."

Jennifer leaned back and smiled broadly. "But not lately," she said. "So let's have another drink, you and me."

Peter sat at the same table where he and Jennifer had had their drinks—to his invitation to have dinner together, she had pleaded fatigue—and he ordered supper: *blanquette de veau*, a salad, wine. The restaurant, about half full (the woman who had been sitting nearby was gone), was exceptionally quiet, and when he was done with his entrée, he ordered a favorite dessert—a *tarte tatin*, carmelized apple pie served upside down—and while he ate the pie and sipped coffee, he found himself remembering the first time he had flown into Durban, and of how, from the plane, the city's harbor had reminded him of Miami Beach: golden beaches, sunbathers, surfers, fishing boats, cruise ships, modern hotels, skyscrapers...

And thinking of Durban, he thought—how not?—of Khuthala, the health care worker who had been his companion during his visit to South Africa the previous summer. Was she still alive? Had she married again? Were her children well?

Khuthala had two teenage daughters, but her husband, who had left four years earlier to work in the diamond mines in Kimberley, had not returned, and she did not expect that he would. Most South African women who were infected have had only one lover, she explained the first time she visited Peter in his apartment. The combination of migrant labor and an industrial

society in which men worked where their labor was needed—
for gold, sugar, diamonds—had proven to be the deadliest of
marriages, for as men moved around the country and, periodi-
cally, returned home, they carried with them the infections they
acquired, which infections they passed on to their wives, who
passed them on to their children. Because of this, and to reas-
sure him that she was one of the lucky ones and had not herself
been HIV-infected, she had, on this first visit, brought her medical records with her.

Peter had responded by telling her that it was a surprise to
the people *he* had worked with in the States, especially during
the years when the AIDS epidemic was exploding, to discover
he was not gay. They called me 'a righteous heterosexual' back
then, he said, and explained the phrase's frame of reference: that
those non-Jews who had helped save Jews during the Second
World War were known as righteous gentiles.

Well, Khuthala had replied, because you came *here* to work, I
already knew you were righteous. And I have certainly been happy to learn that you are, in addition, heterosexual. More exactly,
he recalled her saying—this toward morning of their first night
together—what I'm feeling now is akin to what I suspect you
were feeling when you looked at my medical records: reassured.

That they had been able to give each other mutual reassur-
ances had become the basis of a running joke. If only, they
would suggest after making love, others could be *reassured* in the
way they were, what a kinder, happier world it might be. And
yet, how not at the same time be acutely aware that the act that
gave them enormous pleasure, and comfort, was also the cause
of great suffering and of death.

Morning and evening—before and after work—Peter had
loved walking through the markets with Khuthala, where the
pungent fragrance of a multitude of curries filled the air, and
where most vendors and shoppers were dressed in Indian
garb—in wildly bright and swirling colors that made them look

like enormous parakeets. And walking together to villages and encampments that neither cars nor motorbikes could reach—backpacks and bags of antiretroviral medications with them, and carrying umbrellas to shield themselves from the sun—he had been happy. He had felt something which, in another time and place he would have hesitated to state aloud for fear of being thought pompous, or overly sentimental: that he was once again, as he had been when the AIDS pandemic erupted two decades before, doing the work he believed he had been put on earth to do.

When he let his mind drift back to his three visits to South Africa—a mere seven weeks, in all—and when he saw himself walking across a valley lush with tropical greenery, heading with Zhuthula and two other health care workers to a Zulu compound near the Tugela River—what he could not make sense of was how such a phenomenally beautiful landscape could be home to such a phenomenally deadly disease.

He saw himself in a Zulu compound—one located in the Valley of a Thousand Hills—and he imagined that Jennifer was with him. He imagined that she was explaining how to take the antiretrovirals and how many to take each day and when to take them. He pictured the two of them leaving the hut and being shown, with pride, a stone-fenced cattle crawl in which there was one large cow and a scattering of chickens, and when he recalled the manner in which the people, some holding infants in their arms, had expressed gratitude to them—one hand holding onto the wrist of the hand that, palm upturned, was receiving medications from their hands—he imagined strands of hair falling from their skulls and drifting into the air, skin falling away from their bones in patches, teeth dropping from their mouths and landing one at a time, in soundless puffs of dust, on the dirt of the cattle crawl.

A Missing Year: Letter To My Son

"And so, if the world consisted only of me and you (a notion I was much inclined to have), then this purity of the world came to an end with you, and, by virtue of your advice, the filth began with me."

— Franz Kafka
A Letter To His Father

earest Charlie,

If you are reading this, wherever you are, it will mean, of course, that I am no longer here (there?)—a shame, since when all is said and done, and here I paraphrase Orwell, I find that this world does suit me fairly well. And wherever I am, and unless we've both arrived simultaneously in some universe designed by Calvino or Borges, what I'm certain of is that there is no 'I' there. I never thought to persuade you of that—that when we're gone, we're gone and that's all there is to it, so that the only immortality, as our people (mostly) believe (Jews, but not only Jews—cf. Shakespeare's sonnets), lies in our children, in the memories others have of us, and in whatever work we may have left behind: literary stuff, of course, but *anything* made by one's mind or hands that has tangible existence: music, furniture, boats, paintings, sculpture, jewelry, clothing, houses…

Consciousness is fine—much studied and celebrated in recent times—but much overrated too, in my opinion, for even were it to survive in some way—were we, as in typical tales composed about such after-lives, to wake from death and find that, detached from any bodily being, mind and thought are, miraculously, still ongoing, I would doubtless spend whatever timeless time this 'I'—this consciousness recognizably me and no one else—had been given, lamenting the loss of senses. Taste, touch, sight, sound, smell—smell above all!—how ever, ever, ever undervalue *them*?

I.e., the grave's a fine and private place, as Marvell famously wrote, but none, I think, do there embrace. Other articulations of this notion, along with its innumerable *carpe diem* corollaries about prefering the sybaritic, now accelerate within, creating a rather sweet traffic jam, yet I banish them at once, even as I ask forgiveness for my literary excesses, references, and airs, yes? These musings are—of course, of course—my somewhat arch way of avoiding telling you what I've decided to tell you about what I've always thought of as my 'missing' year—and also a reminder (to me) of how often in this life I've used words on paper to avoid other things. Through most of my life, that is, I've had the largely benign habit of passing whatever I experienced, in mind or flesh, through the filter (lens?) of what, other than you, my son, was the great love of my life: stories.

I tested (tasted?) all I did—my writing, teaching, wives, romances, friendships, pleasures, losses, memories, feelings—all, all, all—through stories I'd read, and people, places, and events I'd come to know in them. More: I often gave myself up as fully as I was able to the imagination of others—let myself believe I was part of the mind—the *sense*-ibility—that had conjured up these worlds so that, I suppose—vain hope!—my own imagination, like theirs, might find objects and tales equal to my desire to find them.

But to the missing year itself: My great fear, you see, was that I would kill you. I *wanted* to kill you. The idea of killing you thrilled and pleased in a time distinctly bereft of thrills or pleasure. For a year—fourteen months and three days, to be exact— I thought, every day, of killing you. The thought arrived, as you might guess, attached to my desire to do away with myself, and this desire arrived shortly *before* your mother left us both (nor, I note quickly, did I ever stoop to blackmailing her with the threat that I would kill the two of us if she *did* leave us). But the desire to kill the two of us came—this dark, unwelcome guest—and it stayed for more than a year, yet could occasionally, when most robust, bring with it (paradoxically?) an exhilarating feeling of liberation.

The possibility of leaving this world, and taking you with me—of being in a place or non-place where consciousness was forever non-existent—this became balm to my pain, and the pain, let me tell you—and I hope you never know it in its dreadful particularity—was decidedly *physical*. During those fourteen months and three days I read a good deal about depression, which, I discovered, had a distinguished history, beginning at least 2500 years ago with Hippocrates, and though the reading taught me much about the melancholic disposition, and about suicidal desires and the pernicious ways they can take hold and take over, I found little about the sheer bodily pain that, as in my case, can accompany the affliction.

Though I experienced most of what have become the standard symptoms that now make major depression certifiable and reimbursable (sleep disturbances, fatigue, feelings of worthlessness, thoughts of suicide), I experienced no weight loss, or loss of sexual desire, no headaches or flu-like symptoms, no sharp internal blade-like grindings. Instead, my lows were accompanied by constant nausea (even—especially!—during love-making), along with a vise-like pressure throughout my upper body, front *and* back, as if I'd been saturated with something heavier than blood—inhabited by a beast that was trying to suck and squeeze breath and life from me. When it came to rising from a bed or chair, the heaviness would at times paralyze me, as if the sheer weight of my body were the palpable equivalent of my spirits.

Aware, however, that what I was experiencing might merely (*merely?!*) be advanced coronary artery disease, I did go to my physician, who forwarded me to a cardiologist, who—hope dashed again—found nothing wrong with my heart, or the arteries that fed it and were fed by it.

Well, I told myself—much as the host of the annual sado-masochist convention is said to have announced—'The good news this year is that we seem to have lots of bad news!' For the cardiologist's evaluation meant that what I was experiencing was, in fact, what I believed it to be: the great black bile itself—melancholic depression.

So there we were, Charlie, abandoned by mother and wife, you having just passed your first birthday—the most beautiful, clever babe ever—and me relieving my newly acquired distress by imagining how sweet it would be to do away with you, and after you—my guilt now boundless!—with me (I spare you details of my how-to fantasies while assuring you that swiftness and lack of suffering for you were paramount in my considerations).

Did I consider murdering your mother? Of course, though not for long, and not at all after I received a kind offer from a former student, a young man from an Italian family in Springfield, Massachusetts, who, learning of my situation, told me he could have a man-with-a-bent-nose (his phrase) take care of things. All I had to do was nod once and it would come to pass in a completely risk-free, cost-free manner.

A mother abandoning a child, he said, was a mean-spirited and irresponsible act that went against both nature and biology, and it would be more than irresponsible—how I adored his repeated use of the word!—not to repair this flaw in the fabric of the world by cleansing it of its perpetrator.

The offer was more than moderately attractive, for among the wealth of evils in human character, meanness-of-spirit and irresponsibility had always, as you know, ranked high in my private catalog. But no matter his assurances (or my desires), I declined the offer. What I feared, you see, was error. I was, that is, afraid of being caught, for being caught—whether for having committed the deed, or having assented to it—would have resulted in your being left to the care of others, and to coping not only with the sequelae of abandonment by a mother (a dead young mother, to boot), but with the burden of having been orphaned by a convicted murderer.

There were comic possibilities here, for sure, though at the time so constant was the animal ache in mind and body that, as with cracked or broken ribs, the mere thought of laughter was enough to lay me out for hours (hmmm: did you know that—sweet memory—you and I shared afternoon nap-time back then, you in your crib, me on my office couch?). The only way I found to escape the constant pain—as undeserving, worthless, wretched, dull, hopeless, lazy, stupid, vain, and homely *shlep* of a man as I'd become—was by imagining the prospect of being somewhere else, and of having you there with me.

Yet there was something else at work in the bowels of my gloom—a fear that arose from my hunger for vengeance: that should I fail to nail my courage to the sticking point in the act itself, *she* would come marching triumphantly back into your life, my deed confirmation of everything she wanted to believe and to have others believe. Plus, a dividend: she'd be the recipient of large quantities of cash, for she'd be seen as the long-suffering mother who'd fled an unhealthy situation—marriage to a dangerous, despicable, deranged man, the proof in the pudding of my murderous intent and botched self-annihilation.

But consequences, Charlie—let us consider consequences. As I would often remind students: if they kept two principles in mind—that character was fate, and that there were no acts without consequences—they could begin to find their way into the workings (and delights) of all tales worthy of attention. When we were home alone, and I pictured our resident would-be Humbert Humbert (me!) mocked by her, I saw, too, the consequences of my inevitable bunglings. Insurance companies do not pay out for death-by-suicide, but her likely appeal—that I was not in my right mind when, at the eleventh hour, I changed beneficiaries (assigning all to charities)—would surely have carried the day. (Actually, I realize, despite a multitude of resolutions, I never did get around to changing *anything* in my will that year, which tells you something about melancholy, and how it can cause a lasting rupture between the desire to act and the ability to act.)

Still, a question: Why did your mother leave us? You were probably hoping—how not?—that in this note you'd find answers, or at least the beginnings of answers. Why she left me— why any woman leaves a man—is rarely, on an overt level, mysterious. There are the usual suspects: She didn't love me, she found me impossible, she wanted her freedom, she fell in love with somebody else, she experienced a sudden change-of-life, she was on alcohol and/or drugs, she found motherhood less than it was cracked up to be, she had a severe, debilitating post-partum chronic depression…

But why she left *you*—ah, to that conundrum, I plead ignorance. While it's true (and sad) that people hardly blink when men leave wives and children, I tend to agree with my Springfield student that when a mother does so, it would seem, in most instances, to go against nature and biology, and therefore, like a miracle—*a miracle!*—be beyond human understanding. For what defined God and God's miracles in the *Old Testament*— from the great flood that covered the earth to the burning bush, from the ten plagues to the sun standing still in the heavens— were occurrences that, *by definition*, went against nature and the natural order, and could, thus, have been brought about only by a god who was transcendent and (also by definition) beyond our understanding.

When people asked why she left you, and would suggest, thinking this would console me, that perhaps she'd suffered some kind of mental breakdown, I'd nod knowingly, as if the suggestion had merit, and say that perhaps what troubled your mother could be found in the psychiatric encyclopedia of mental disorders—the infamous *DSM*—under the letter A. Under 'A?' they'd ask. Yes, I'd say: A… for 'Absence of Character.'

How else respond to such a foolish question? Still, you must wonder at times about what she (this woman you never truly knew) was like, and, allied to this question, what I *saw-in-her* that led to love, marriage, and bringing you into the world.

And the answer?

Simple: We were young, she was beautiful, and she told me—insecure, neurotic young Jewish boy that I was—that she loved me. You've seen pictures, of course, but they don't begin to capture the seductive *wholesomeness* of her beauty: a blond-haired, blue-eyed, corn-fed Midwesterner (from Iowa: the heart of corn country)—a cheerful cheerleader with a perfect gleaming American smile and a perpetual blush in her cheeks, crossed with a full-bodied, voluptuous Scandinavian (think: Liv Ullman, Anita Ekberg)—an exquisitely desirable woman who, after she'd told me she loved me, said two additional things that sealed the deal: first, that she believed—she knew, she just *knew!*—I was going to become a truly *great* writer; and second, that I was the most wonderful lover she'd ever known.

And let me tell you, son, as I discovered too late in the game, when it came to the latter, she knew whereby she spoke. But (sigh!) even irony and distance cannot keep away the return, in memory, of the excruciating feelings of hurt, shame, and helplessness that came with my discovery of her several lovers, which news was soon followed by her leave-taking, which act itself (the better miracle, for it gave us our years together, you and me) was preceded, as I noted above, by the arrival of a constant, gnawing pain, along with sensations of a kind I'd never before known: I kept falling into a darkness more terrifying than the absence of the dimmest light—into a hole that was at the same time somehow a hollow *within me*, so that I felt I was disappearing into myself again and again, and without any clue as to how to stop—or name!—the falling.

To give you an inkling (ink link?) of how my baleful innocence was destroyed: we were to meet for lunch at the university's Faculty Club, and I arrived early (to have twenty minutes or so in which to rework a lecture I was preparing on Henry James-the-Irishman), went to the men's room to wash up, heard a strange guttural sound, found the stall where the sound was coming from, opened the door, and there was your mother, skirt up around her waist, sitting astride a young man—he worked as a busboy at the club—who was himself sitting on an open toilet, his pants gathered around his ankles. 'Good afternoon, Professor Klein,' he said, with great good manners. 'Sorry to see you here so early today.' And your mother, over her shoulder, her eyes filled with lust-fulfilled bliss, 'Oh Sam, we really do have to stop meeting like this…'

I hurried home from the Faculty Club, and when she joined me, and when I wept and said the obvious—bad enough that you were doing it, but you *knew* I would be there—*We had a date!*—she said of course she knew—that was the point, after all, for didn't this *non*-coincidence answer the pertinent questions? But I was a helpless, wounded beggar—distraught, destroyed, disabled. The rage, and its faithful companion, clinical depression, were to come later, though I don't think she sensed this, or ever gave such possibilities much thought. On that afternoon, however, she did for a while sit beside me, stroke my hair, and wipe my tears away. What I think, she said before she left, is that I was trying to get your attention.

The rest—what I knew and when I knew it—is theme and variation, and my conclusion is that it turned out to be our great good fortune that once she left, she never returned. Her life, such as it became, is a void too—a mystery—though of decreasing interest. Out of sight became, literally, out of mind. Another conclusion, perhaps a trifle too generous on my part: that her intention was not to humiliate me, but more simply (mindless-ly?) to please herself. The shameless narcissism—the unthinking sense of entitlement of an unusually beautiful, and, then as now (*pace* Orwell's warning about double-negatives), not unintelligent woman, seemed a not unnatural phenomenon.

There were annual birthday cards from her to you, the last when you were twelve, but the envelopes were without return addresses, and I chose not to give you the cards. Why stir up unanswerable questions, or feelings that were beyond gratification? I myself had several New Year's cards from her, with un-characteristically bland greetings: 'with love' or 'kind regards' or 'wishing you a year of health, happiness, and adventure'—and also a letter congratulating me on the publication of my novel, *Prizefighter*, hoping it would be the first of many successes (as of this writing, there has never been a successor—her hope, then, become a curse that I embraced?), and noting that the scene in which the protagonist discovers his girlfriend has cheated on him suggested to her that I had not yet gotten over what she saw as inconsequential dalliances of a kind that occurred in most—her word—*mature* marriages. 'Grow up, Sam,' she advised.

Once she left, she never inquired about you. But if she had, I might have informed her that instead of killing you, or her, or myself, I had decided to live, and that it was you, Charlie—her son—who, unwittingly, saved *all* our lives. You didn't know that, did you?

How it happened: I had begun drinking even before your mother left us. On a daily basis, the numbing of senses—along with the resultant dizziness, fogged mind, and clogged sleep—got me through. I'd pour a bit of Scotch (Dewar's) into my cof-fee at the start of the day; while receiving students in my office, I'd fill and refill a mug from a flask I kept in my bottom-right desk drawer; and when I arrived home I'd treat myself to the drink I told myself I was entitled to after a long day's work. On teaching days I left you in a nursery school, three blocks away, run by two Amherst College faculty wives, both of whom, on random occasions, without, as far as I know, their sharing confidences, I plowed royally, despite or because of the alcohol that had me working hard not to call them, in the throes, by one another's names.

But what your mother called her 'dalliances'—and what a colleague who'd been one of those favored by her generosity called her 'open-legs policy,' a policy that favored at least two other department colleagues (a 'most favored nations policy?'), along with perhaps three of my male graduate students, and two female undergraduate honors students (to her credit, she did not discriminate on the basis of age, gender, or race)—utterly destroyed me. In her presence, hoping to get some purchase on what seemed an increasingly fragile world—an apology perhaps, a vow to reform and start over, an acknowledgement of the effect of her actions on me, a suggestion that we sign up for couples counseling—I was all fumbling and trembling. The only thing I wanted was to save our marriage and family, to make her stop having lovers, and to have her love me again.

But I *do* love you, she would say. And really, Sam, why the surprise? Haven't you always said that the great thing in life was to remain *open to possibility* (a phrase I had, to my chagrin, used frequently during our courtship, especially when in pursuit of specific physical attentions)?

Didn't I agree, given our mutual love of sensuality—of polymorphous perversity—that the prospect of making love with one person and one person only for the next half century was absurd? Didn't I see that her act had been a gift, and would enable us, *dans le style français*, to remain *together* for the duration? Moreover, your mother declared, what she did when she was not at home was *her private life*, and hadn't I, in at least two essays about the decline of the novel from its cultural centrality, linked this decline to the parallel (and lamentable) decline in our valuation of privacy?

Her words—the news, the facts—fell on tender ears, and on a sensibility—and ego—too blue and bruised to bear them. I was a failure—as husband, father, man—and would never recover from what everyone would surely see as well-earned punishment. Her arguments, such as they were (to her credit, she never attempted to *convince* me of anything), though I could acknowledge their merits, passed me by.

What did *not* pass by was the knowledge that I had turned out to be much more a man of my generation and upbringing than I had acknowledged—'distressingly conventional,' was your mother's judgment—for I had clearly (and mistakenly) believed that if vows of love and marriage were exchanged, like the bodily intimacies that were their physical manifestations, they were intended to be honored eternally. Although your mother and I were born of the same generation, she had somehow escaped—evolved from?—values of fidelity I, and most people I grew up with, had pledged obedience to. I couldn't, that is, bear knowing that what she gave to me, she bestowed freely (happily?) on others. In me, I discovered, jealousy easily trumped rationality, even though I knew—could proclaim—that jealousy was itself merely the illusion of possession.

But oh my, the power of that illusion in my imagination. At first, all I wanted was for her to forgive me, for me to forgive her, for her to forgive me for my difficulty in forgiving her, et cetera et cetera. But when—to test me?—she suggested we have her favorite graduate student (not the busboy, but another) move in with us—he could, she argued, help with you, Charlie, and with chores (feedings, diapers, babysitting, lawn mowing), and help us renew what clearly, to judge from my upset, was in need of renewal. When I said no—no, never, *jamais, mai, nunca, nunquam*, over my dead body—*genug!*—she simply smiled, said I could have things my way, and left. I didn't see her for the next four days or nights, and these were the first evenings, and mornings, when my closest friend became Dewar's. In fact, on the fifth morning after her absence, she found me on the bathroom floor, lying in my puke while you wailed away in your crib.

Though you're pitiable, she said (she used the French *pénible*, a deft touch, thereby connoting both pitiable *and* pathetic, and helping the dagger of her betrayal to penetrate more easily), I don't pity you, and I certainly don't want to listen to that little lump of flesh and diarrhea (a reference to you, son) crying all day. So I'm out of here, Sam.

I managed to get to my feet and wash my face, and she smiled at me with what seemed genuine kindness: We gave it our best, she said. I believe we really did. But it's not for me, this marriage-mommy thing, and better that we know it sooner than later, wouldn't you agree?

I agreed, of course. Yes, I said. Oh sure. Of course. *Bien sûr*. Whatever you say. Whatever you *want*! And then we were two, and I picked you up, set you down on the changing table, changed your diaper, and rocked you in my arms, and thought, were this a story, what suggestion could I make that would lend it credibility, or, better still, sympathy for its protagonist? And as soon as I asked, the answer was there—the old writer's standby, courtesy of Messrs. Twain and Faulkner: You must kill your darlings.

The fantasy, along with drink, did, as I said earlier, help get me through. What part of me believed, you see, was that the best and only way to get back at her and hurt her *badly* was to hurt *you* (her son, after all). But no Medea, *moi*—and, give thanks to whatever gods that be, no Greek tragedy in the House of Klein either. At the time I didn't think through the idea of doing away with us, or believe in it—it seemed, simply, the only solution to ending the pain, which dragged with it a thunderous noise that had taken to traveling in a continual, merciless loop through the marrow of my bones.

In truth, I don't think I believed much of anything that year, which may be why it seems missing. And it has always seemed missing, obviously, because *I* was missing—in action, and in *in*-action. Though I try now and then to summon up memories—*à la recherche*, Sam, I cry out silently; *à la recherche!*—I recall few details: I slept, I ate, I taught, I shaved, I pissed, I shat, and I drank; I shopped, I cooked, I fed us, I put you to sleep, I took you to nursery school, I picked you up from nursery school, I took you to the doctor, I talked to you, I talked *with* you, I bought you clothes, I dressed you, I changed your diapers, I toilet-trained you, I helped you learn to walk and to ride a tricycle, and I probably took some delight in your development. You were the best and brightest of them all, the nursery school ladies told me, as did a coterie of grad student babysitters (several of whom offered to stay the night, invitations I wisely, though not without ambivalence, declined): before you were fifteen months old, you could play simple games of cards ('War,' 'Go-Fish'), pick out favorite CDs, sing songs on-key and hold to your part in rounds, ice-skate on double runners, and laugh at jokes. You were also enormously responsive, affectionate, and trusting, though given our circumstances, who can figure why.

A for-instance: Once, putting you to bed at night, a glass of Jim Beam in hand (seven and a half months following your mother's departure, in a decision I considered to be a mark of incipient maturity, I had switched from Scotch to bourbon), you asked for a taste, and I dipped my finger in, let you lick it.

So what's your daddy's favorite drink? I asked, and when you looked puzzled, I gave you the answer: Why, the *next* one, of course—!

You cracked up—a bubbling belly laugh that had you clapping your hands and rolling around in your crib. Did you understand the joke? Were you just being silly? Were you reacting to the way I was laughing at my own joke? Were you laughing because you thought laughing would please me...?

Six weeks and two days after your first birthday, I received papers from a lawyer, informing me that your mother wanted nothing from me except my agreement to a divorce, and to be able to retrieve some personal possessions. In this, I suppose, her behavior was admirable. If I agreed not to contest the divorce, we could take legal and permanent leave of each other within ninety days, with no monies or properties exchanged or owed.

It was done, and the finality of documents and signatures, once processed and approved by a court, went a long way in helping to thicken the heavy, sooty fog in which I lived. No matter what words I or anyone put on it, let me tell you: there is nothing as awful as feeling so deeply sad that to leave the world seems not only, in prospect, a relief, but *just*! How much better life would be for everyone else were I gone! What a gift to the world my absence would be! But if I did it solo, I feared, she would get you, or, if she demurred, the courts would get you, and such thoughts also held me back.

And there was also time—the *passage* of time, more exactly. At some point in the thirteenth month of my sorrows, the beast inside mind and body seemed to tire of me a bit (out of boredom, I hypothesized), and I noticed, too, that I was taking occasional pleasure from simple things—eating, sleeping, holding your hand on walks, watching you eat, or sleep, or play with your toy cars and building blocks—and I began to have a distaste, not for bourbon—never, never, never—but for the foggy dizziness it induced. Then you fell.

I was, as usual, moderately sloshed, and it was your bedtime, and I had a stack of papers to grade, a few rolled and tucked snugly under my left arm, and I was *very* upset with you because you'd soiled yourself. *Why?* Why were you doing this to me? You'd been toilet-trained for six or seven weeks, we'd both taken pride in the achievement, and you'd graduated from your crib to a bed—the top half of the old hi-riser that had served as *my* childhood bed. Why *now*? Had I not been paying you enough attention? Were you angry with me? Were you missing your mother, or one of our babysitters (you'd taken an especial shine to a vixenish young woman named Robyn Henderson, who, by infiltrating your affections, was determined to have your father infiltrate her moist, secret places), or...

Who knew? What I do know is that when I smelled the presence of the foul deed, and asked if you had done it, I was already too angry for anyone's good, and when you grinned with a fiendish look of feigned innocence, and said, 'I don't *know*, Daddy,' I lost it.

So I did what I did sometimes: I let loose with words as if I were battering a punching bag with them—How many times have I told you this or that, and What's the matter with you, you ungrateful little *schmuck*, and When the fuck are you going to grow up, and I have no patience left for you, and additional choice and self-pitying gabble about having to do everything, everything, everything by myself. Give me a break, you little shit-head, you and your shit-filled pants! I screamed. Just give me a fucking break, you stupid lump of clumped, rotten turds! In my fury, and without at first letting go of the student papers, I grabbed you—*snatched* you—and carried you in the crook of my right arm up the stairs and into your room, where I tried to hoist you up onto the changing table. But the flight of stairs had made the bourbon produce a major shimmer of nausea—Hey, I wanted to shout to the world: Look at the noble, dead drunk dumb daddy doing his goddamned dumb thing!—and as I lifted you with the intent of slamming you down on the table—smashing you!—you slipped out of my grasp, and for an instant, as in the memory of car crashes, all went into sickly slow motion: I saw you falling, and I saw that your head had turned upside down, and that the exposed and sharp iron corner of your bed was in perfect position to receive your skull—and yet you smiled at me with the most loving, trusting smile I had ever seen or expect ever to see again.

You had no fear, Charlie. You seemed to believe that if I were taking care of you, no harm could come your way. How ever, ever forget your sublime calm—the loving trust in your eyes?

I dropped the student papers, scooped you up before you hit the bed's flanged corner ('A fumble recovered, folks!' I heard an announcer proclaim), cleaned you up, and dressed you in freshly laundered pajamas. 'Sorry, Daddy,' you said and, when you noticed the glimmering film in my eyes, you asked if I'd hurt myself.

Not at all, I said. Not at all.

I stopped drinking the next morning. The glooms retreated, defeated by your trust in me, which was, in that moment, certainly greater than *my* trust in me. Three weeks later, I received galleys for *Prizefighter*, and you and I celebrated by driving to Maine for lunch (clam rolls became your favorite food well into your teens). I waded into revisions with gusto, and within a year I married again—Inez Palenco, a sweet, bright woman four years older than I (a social worker at an agency in Holyoke, a competent oboist, and a master gardener), whom you may remember only through photos, for within seventeen months of our marriage, she was done in by that cunning variety of breast cancer that can sneak in and take over *between* regular check-ups.

Somehow you grew up, went to school, graduated, and set off to seek your fortune, and what I have since thought of as The Great Glooms never returned with any marked force, though I feared their return, as now, every day when I woke and every night before I slept—and you turned into as fine a son as any man might be lucky enough to have.

Let me note something else that contributed to the fading away of my missing year, and I note it not to deprive you of credit for having helped me—us!—come to a better place, but to put what happened, and how it happened, into a somewhat larger context. I had, perhaps two years before the night on which you fell, come under the spell of Primo Levi, who, as man and writer, had become my hero. As you know, he wrote about his experiences in Auschwitz and journey home from Auschwitz, but also about myriad other matters: his career as a chemist, his family, other people's vocations, his friendships, his beloved city of Turin.

It has occurred to me of late—when I have, happily, been able to give freer rein to my ruminative disposition—that the slight lessening of depressive pain I began to experience may have come from reading, not about Levi's life as victim, survivor, and witness, but about his views on suicide, along with what in him is so life-affirming (to use an apt if banal phrase): his fierce ability to see the differences in other people—their particularities and idiosyncracies—in a time when they were put to death because they were judged, as Jews, to be *no* different, one from the other.

Though, of course, they were also exterminated because they were just that: *other*. We always fear, and despise, whatever we perceive as different from who we are, and in this, he has explained, we are not that different from animals, who are much more intolerant of members of their own species than they are of those of other species. Thus, anti-Semitism, he has suggested, is simply a horrific example of a more general phenomenon.

But suicide—what about suicide? There were, I was surprised to learn, few suicides in the camps—and generally, Levi points out, fewer suicides in wartime than in times of peace. His reasoning as to why this was so appears in a self-interview I came across a few evenings before the night on which you fell, and long before—inexplicable, profoundly disturbing mystery!—*he* fell down a stairwell in a self-willed act I trust neither of us will emulate—one that ended his life in the place he loved: the house in which he'd been born and, before and after Auschwitz, had lived.

Yet some years before this, Levi wrote that he considered suicide a distinctively human act (we had never seen evidence that animals committed suicide), and that because, in the camps, human beings, both victims and oppressors, tended more toward the level of animals—of *animality*—it was the business of the day—essentials—that ruled: what you were going to eat and if you were going to eat, how cold it would be, what you would wear against the cold, how heavy was the work and of what kind, et cetera. In short: you thought, if 'thought' is the right word, of how you were going to make it through the day and into the evening and through the night. There was, simply, no time to think about killing yourself.

So I became busy. I began exercising regularly. I began preparing, in earnest, for the book I would write about Henry James as Irishman; I began making notes for new stories and novels; I began planting a garden, and learning carpentry; I began seeking out women who would make suitable helpmates for me, and loving (step-)mothers for you. I began cooking meals regularly, breakfast and dinner, and planning vacations, and asking my department chair if I could teach new courses that would require I put myself to school in the work of authors (Howells, Dos Passos, Proust, Beckett) with whom I had, until then, only cursory acquaintance. I took tennis lessons, joined a co-ed softball team, took a course in auto repair, and searched out (in vain for the most part) lost cousins, aunts, and uncles. I painted rooms, repaired furniture, built bookcases, created file systems, learned to do my own taxes, and to play the piano.

Not all at once, of course, and after a while—when the demon of depression seemed to have increasing difficulty finding its way back into my daily life, I began to let some of the new activities fall away. But this happened over the course of several years, and I mark what has, until this moment, been its *definitive* departure (though daily *wariness* remains), from the third month of my third marriage—to Pamela Fullerton, whom you will recall as perhaps the most animated and lively of my five wives, though herself—the aphrodisiacal cue and clue to my infatuation and our romance?—a lifelong victim of chronic depression, which, in the glory days of falling in love, departed, only to return when a bit of the bloom, as was inevitable, began to wear off the rose of our bliss.

Pamela never became suicidal—her condition was more like a ground bass, or low-grade hum—a Baroque ostinato I came to think I could actually *hear*, and some twenty-one months after our wedding, she left us, saying it was simply not fair—not *fair*!—can you *imagine*?—that it was *not fair* for anyone to have to live with someone so plagued with sadness, and with such catastrophic changes of mood. (Why, she would write in a note a month or two later, should we have to live *our* lives on the nauseating sine-curve of *her* feelings?)

I tried to talk her out of leaving (I truly loved her, as, in fact, I loved *all* my wives, along with a good number of my girlfriends; my capacity for falling in love, and staying in love, being one of my more consistent capabilities), and with medications (not then as effective as they are said to be now), and some psychotherapy, she did return to her happier and more stable self for a while. Her will to be a miserable, unloved, unworthy, abandoned child, however, proved ultimately stronger than medications, therapy, or us. In the cartons of correspondence I have left behind, you will, if interested, find some four to five dozen letters from Pamela. She never married again, never had children, and always inquired about you, Charlie. I believe she missed you more than she missed me, the fact that you were and were not her (only) son creating complex, and somewhat anguished attachments, not to you—no guilt, Charlie, please, please!—but to parts of her earlier life that held a power over her against which all efforts, ours included—tolerant and loving though we both were—proved helpless.

But to the end of ending this meditation, let me return to what I saw in your eyes, and believe I sensed of your sensibility—and thus, your happy prospects—on the night of your fall. I had, then as now, the highest hopes for you, Charlie, and I trust you won't confuse these hopes for expectations. Of the latter, I have none. Let me explain: When I was preparing my book on Henry James, I came across a letter Mrs. Cadwalader Jones wrote to a friend after having come upon some of James's early stories. The stories were pleasing, and well enough made, she wrote. What had impressed, though, was that the stories were informed, despite their undistinguished quality *as stories*, by a remarkable and remarkably unexpected singularity of mind— a quality of mind so rare it had taken her by surprise, and moved her utterly. It is so difficult, she wrote (in a sentence with which I've always hoped—no: intended!—to end this letter)—it is so difficult to do anything well in this mysterious world.

Comfort

The previous afternoon, when they were less than a two hour drive from Le Tignet, a small village in the south of France, they had turned off *Nationale 95*—the old *Route Napoléan*—and meandered through towns and villages that seemed little changed since they had passed this way in 1968.

Now, drinking coffee on a terrace that overlooked the Lac de Castillon, Saul found himself remembering how, during the time they lived in Le Tignet, they had adopted the custom once a week of searching out a new town or village, usually one they had read about in *Les Plus Beaux Villages de France*. They would start out after breakfast, arrive at their destination within an hour or two, wander the village's streets, enjoy a leisurely lunch, and after lunch adjourn to a local hotel where they would, before returning home, make love.

The names of the villages stayed with him—Gordes, Séguret, Ménerbes, Ansouis, Coaraze, Peillon—and there were others, not included in *Les Plus Beaux Villages*, they had happened upon and, by doing so, made their own: Sisteron, Draguignan, Digne, Rousillon, Gap, Mons, Eze, Bonnieux, Ys, Apt—each name having the power, still, to evoke specific days, conversations, meals, and rooms. In Digne, he recalled, in the Hotel de Ville, the wallpaper had been composed of faded red and green chevrons like those on Chevrolets; in Peillon, they had, within less than a minute of entering their room, and with most of their clothes on, made love, and they had done so standing up,

Janice's back against the door, her legs clasped around his thighs; in Ménerbes, they had talked for the first time about getting married; in Apt, on a noisy, broken-springed bed, he had—another first—entered her from behind; and on a broiling August day in Entrevaux, in a room with a large chestnut armoire, one whose doors were faced with narrow gilded mirrors covered with colored streaks that, in memory, appeared to be dried blood stains, they had, after love-making, and on sweat-drenched sheets, fallen into the blackest, most sublime post-coital sleep he had ever experienced.

Was the hotel still here?

While Janice talked about their daughter Ellen, who had, several weeks before their departure, taken up with a guy Janice said was like the others: an untrustworthy, manipulative drifter, Saul thought about Camus. It was because of Camus—of his reading of Camus's *The Plague*—that Saul had, forty years before, while they were living in Le Tignet, decided to become a doctor. This had happened—this small epiphany that changed the course of his life—in May of 1968 when the entire French nation was shut down by striking students and workers, a time when he and Janice had believed that a revolution was taking place in France that had the potential to transform the world. They had arrived in France the previous summer, ten days after graduating from Oberlin College, and seven weeks after having voted themselves a year in which to travel in Europe before returning to the States, and before making decisions about jobs, careers, and family.

So that Janice would think he shared her concern about Ellen, Saul asked questions—Was the guy doing drugs? Was he abusive? Did he have a day job? Was he *clean*?—though his mind was not on Ellen, but on his imagined affinities with Camus, a man who had once declared that he believed in three things only—in courage, in intelligence, and in women. On his last day on earth, while riding in the car in which, at the age of forty-eight, he would be killed, Camus, in a kind of a premonitory revelation that Saul envied, had told his friends, Janine and Michel Gallimard (Michel was Camus's publisher), that he felt he had made all his women happy, even those he had loved simultaneously.

Janice was asking when, after they spent some time in Le Tignet, they might begin traveling again—Saul had promised they would go to Italy: Venice, Florence, Siena—and Saul said he couldn't think about that yet. Why so intent on planning? Why not just let things happen? Couldn't they simply be where they were without thinking of where they *might* be?

Janice sighed. "Look, I'm not trying to organize your life, much less run it," she said. "In truth, you seem so distracted that I was just making conversation. I thought that talking about Ellen might have upset you."

"Let's enjoy the view, okay?" Saul said. "As for Ellen, she's been down this road before. She'll tire of the guy in a month or so, and go on to another."

"And if she continues in her patterns? Can you imagine her going on like this through her thirties and forties?"

"I'm not into imagining what might be," he said. "Ellen's Ellen. I don't imagine her being anyone else."

He looked away, toward the lake, its surface gray, calm, metallic. He pictured Camus leaving Villeblevin and driving south along *Nationale 5* until he came to the spot some twenty-four kilometers north of Sens (was the *Nationale 5* still there?; Saul had not been able to find it on the new map he'd bought), where the car Camus was traveling in with his friends and their eighteen-year-old daughter Anne, along with the Gallimards's dog, had slammed into a tall plane tree, bounced off, then crashed into another tree some forty feet beyond the first.

Although neither his face nor body showed signs of visible injury, Camus, his skull fractured and neck broken, had been killed instantly. Michel Gallimard died five days later while being operated on for a brain hemorrhage. Neither Janine, who was found near her husband, leash in hand, calling for the dog, nor Anne, who was found sitting in a field some sixty-five feet from the crash, were seriously hurt. Camus's black leather briefcase, which contained his passport, photographs, and some books—including Nietsche's *Le Gai Savoir* and a school edition of *Othello*, along with a manuscript of what would be his posthumously published novel, *Le Premier Homme*—survived intact.

Camus had written, previous to this day, that he considered death in an automobile to be *une morte imbécile*—the single most absurd way of dying. The manner of Camus's death, thus, made sense to Saul. But to visit the spot where Camus had died—or even to stop in Villeblevin or Lourmarin, as Janice, in deference to Saul's obsession with Camus, had suggested—was not something he cared to put on their itinerary.

They came upon the village of Entrevaux the way they had first come upon it forty years before, from the east, and once again—suddenly, physically—it took Saul's breath away. Janice, hearing his rasped intake of air, pulled to the side of the road, turned off the engine.

"Are you all *right*?" she asked.

He stepped from the car, rested his hand on his chest, felt loud, irregular thumpings, and heard, also, the sound of rushing water. He wondered, for an instant, if the sound were coming from within—if his blood pressure were rising immoderately. In the silence, though—unearthly somehow, as if they had been transported to a place covered with a huge transparent dome, one that let *in* light, but that kept *out* all sound—it occurred to him, with relief, that the sound of rushing water probably *was* the sound of water: of the Var River, which, overflowing from spring rain and mountain run-off, would be surging nearby.

The village seemed, as ever, an apparition: from a cluster of perhaps a hundred closely set stone-walled houses that seemed to grow from the ground itself, their red tile roofs bright in the late morning sun, a walled road zigzagged up the side of a pyramid-shaped mountain. At the top, some fifteen hundred feet above ground level, was a medieval fortress from whose ramparts one had a three-hundred-sixty-degree view of the surrounding countryside.

"I'm excited is all," Saul offered. "It's just very *exciting* to be here again."

"We should eat," she said.

"And then—?"

They walked toward the part of town where they expected to find the hotel they had once stayed in and where, were it open, they would have lunch. The village seemed preternaturally quiet, shutters on most homes closed while people ate their mid-day meals and prepared for their siestas. They remembered this: that stores in these villages—butcher shops, bakeries, groceries— closed down for two to three hours mid-day, and all afternoon on Wednesdays.

They found their way to the far side of the village, walked along a path that bordered the Var River, and came to an abandoned fortress. Beside its drawbridge, a few feet from the river's bank, three small green-backed turtles sat on a single flat rock. Under the bridge, where the river narrowed, the water, coursing downstream, foamed with increased turbulence, and he thought of boiling water, and of the fact that if you placed a frog in a pot of boiling water, it would jump out, but if you put it in the same pot, and then lit a fire underneath the pot and let the water come to a boil slowly, the frog would remain where it was, and would die.

He had often mentioned this fact to his medical students even before, he would joke during lectures, Al Gore had 'expropriated' it for his film on global warming, and he had used the fact in order to draw his students' attention to the ways in which human beings, like frogs, seemed to have been programmed by evolution to be able to respond to acute crises but not to chronic conditions, not to thinking and acting in terms of long-range effects and consequences.

This short-sightedness was deadly when it came to medical care, where the government, medical groups, insurance companies, and his own hospital rarely thought long-term, where the premium was always on efficiencies dictated by profit margins and cost-effective ratios, and where, therefore, doctors were paid more for procedures—to shove things down people's mouths or up their assholes—than they were for essentials, like taking good histories.

It was the same, he'd come to think, with matters beyond health care: the belief that we were going to have a quick, neat, and complete victory in Iraq—to shock and awe the enemy without having to think about or deal with the aftermath of our invasion; the delusion that we could keep polluting and using up the world's resources—water, air, oil, coal, minerals, wetlands, forests—without regard to consequences and future generations.

And so, when the Bush administration had pushed for a delay in giving grants to the UN Global AIDS Fund—of an amount that was, as a percentage of Gross National Product, the lowest amount *any* developed nation was contributing—he had gone to his office, told the nursing staff to hold all calls, and, feeling like the Moses Herzog of the AIDS pandemic, written a letter to the president in which he identified himself as an AIDS doctor, and accused the president of being a murderer. For if, he had written, you watch a neighbor drowning and you have a life preserver and do not throw the life preserver to that neighbor, you have killed that person, which was what, when it came to AIDS, we were doing. Unlike Moses Herzog, however, who rarely sent his missives off, Saul had left his office and put the letter in the nearest mailbox.

In the letter's final version, he had edited out an appeal to self-interest: the deadly truth, given that viruses were now frequent flyers—passengers moving around the globe with astonishing speed—that what happened in South Africa, South America, South East Asia, or the South Pacific affected *us*. We were, none of us, islands entire unto ourselves, and we were none of us safe. Whatever spread across poor nations would eventually spread across wealthy nations. It behooved us then, for our *own* well-being, to think of others, to think long-term, and to be generous. It was better, that is, and in the most literal way, to give than to receive.

So that what Saul hoped to do during his mini-sabbatical of four months was to explore and write about why it was we seemed destined never, as a species, to think in our own long-term interests. Was there some underlying biological reason for this inability to respond to conditions that had the potential to destroy us? Did we possess some kind of innate biological death-wish that would lead, inevitably, to our destruction?

The questions, he believed, if obvious, were the ones to ask. How and where he would find anything resembling answers, though, was beyond him. We did not respond to the familiar *because* it was familiar—because it was regular, predictable, and did not *appear* dangerous. That much he had figured out. Also: that people became excited about *crises*—an anthrax scare, a tsunami, SARS—acute incidents in which somebody was done in by a can of contaminated food or a bottle of adulterated pills. As for insurance companies, why should they think long-term when the clients they were serving now would probably not be the clients they would be serving a year or two from now?

But AIDS—medically, epidemiologically, politically—was hardly predictable or ordinary. There must, therefore, he believed, be some biological reason for our inability to respond to it in a sane, sensible, and *self-interested* way. He was not, however, a biologist, an animal behaviorist, an epidemiologist, or an anthropologist. Nor did he know much about what would, in this instance, probably be the most useful disciplines: sociobiology and evolutionary medicine.

What he *did* know was AIDS. He knew, clinically and from the literature, its toll—past, present, and future. Still, if he found answers—if he *could* write a book that would be the equivalent for the twenty-first century of what Camus's book had been for the second half of the twentieth, what then? Had *The Plague* changed anything?

Janice, a clinical psychologist who worked as a consultant to school districts while maintaining a small private practice, had thought the letter foolish—a transparently childish attempt to get himself punished, and further proof that he was losing it: that he was overworked and depressed, and that his years of caring for AIDS patients had finally done him in. He couldn't disagree, for until the last few years, when a new generation of antiretrovirals had, blessedly, proven effective, every last one of the thousands of AIDS patients he had tended to during the previous two decades had died.

But even before the AIDS pandemic had exacerbated what Janice saw as Saul's considerable capacity for survivor guilt, she had frequently remarked on the obvious: his tendency to dwell not on those patients whose sufferings he had ameliorated, or whose lives he had saved, but—always, always—on those he had lost.

What he also hoped to do during his leave—thus his acquiescing to Janice's insistence that he take the mini-sabbatical the medical school had offered—was to try to repair their marriage, though given how far each of them had strayed in recent years, he doubted this was possible. Still, returning to a place where they had been happy once upon a time, might, they both agreed, help, for it did remain true—a tangible basis for hope?—that they had stayed together for more than forty years in a time when most people they knew—friends, relatives, colleagues— had long ago divorced and moved on to new couplings, new marriages.

Saul watched the turtles slide from the rock and disappear into the river, one following the other, and only when the third one was gone did he become aware that Janice had, and for some time, been leaning against him, her hand on his shoulder.

Walking back through town, they stopped in front of a larger building—Hotel du Midi—not the hotel they had once stayed in, but another—to read signs taped to the hotel's door: a hand-written note from the *propriétaires*, Monsieur and Madame Bruno (the hotel and restaurant would be open again from May 15 to September 15); from the village's church (times for Sunday Mass and weekday services); from the mayor's office (times that water would be turned off; rules concerning sheep, goats, pigeons, and dogs); and—what had caught Saul's eye—a poster announcing a concert by The Turetzky Duo, to be held in Grasse at the *Maison de Jeunesse et de Culture*.

"Didn't we hear them in Boston a few years back?" Janice asked.

"Yes. But they were a trio then. The Turetzky Trio. The violinist and the cellist were brothers. The pianist was the cellist's wife."

"She wore a full-length, low-cut gown—burgundy, I recall, with black lace trim," Janice said. "And they performed my favorite—the Schubert 'B flat Trio.' She was an exceptionally beautiful woman."

"Was she?"

"As if you wouldn't notice," Janice said. "Tell me, Saul—we're alone, nobody else will hear—but have you *ever* met a beautiful woman you didn't remember?"

"Probably not," he said.

Entrevaux had only three passageways that could legitimately be called streets, only one of which was wide enough to allow for automobiles, so that when they had circled back to their car a third time without having encountered anyone from the village, or found the hotel, Janice suggested they move on.

"Does anyone live here anymore?" she asked.

"I heard a dog bark," Saul said.

"Do you remember, when we first read through the *Plus Beaux Villages* book, how I noticed that there were rarely people in the photos?" she asked.

"Yes."

"Yes *what*?"

"Yes, I remember you noticed that. You said that the villages seemed very beautiful, and very dead."

"I'd forgotten, too, once you're inside these villages, how little light gets through," Janice said. "All the alleyways and narrow streets, the thick walls without windows—"

"To keep out cold and wind in winter," Saul said, "and to keep out sun and heat in summer. Also to protect against invasions. In villages like this—*villages perchés*—most of the windows to the outside were added in the years *after* the villages had lost their military role."

"My scholar," Janice said.

"Don't mock, please."

"Are you hungry?" she asked.

She pressed herself against him, lightly, and nibbled at his ear. He did not push her away.

"Can we go, please?" he asked.

He opened the car door, but before getting in he stepped behind Janice and nuzzled her, his mouth on the nape of her neck. Her skin was warm and salty, and he considered lifting her skirt and doing her from behind—he was confident they could, close to the car, bring this off while seeming to be embracing—but as he bit at her neck, he found himself troubled momentarily by his anger. Was his sudden desire to hurt her, he wondered, greater than his desire *for* her? But, as often happened, he found, too, that he was soon comforted—his ardor and rage compromised—by what had become a heartening, familiar thought: that though H.I.V. and AIDS would be with us for the rest of human history, he would not.

The Debt

You will doubtless be surprised to hear from me after so many years, she had written. She wished she had been able to send the check long before this, she explained, not so that their accounts could be settled—that was hardly her intent—but so that she might, for her part—she wouldn't presume to speak for him— feel, at last, that what they had decided, and done, once upon a time, had been truly and equally shared. What she continued to long for in this life—was it the same for him?—was mutuality: an easy, ongoing mutuality.

She had apologized for the awkwardness of her phrasings— yes, despite her seeming (and practiced!) air of self-confidence, she found herself, still, feeling helplessly self-conscious the in- stant she put words on paper that he would see—after which she filled him in on the basics of her life since they had last seen each other: her three children were grown and married; she had five grandchildren; she had been a widow for more than seven years; she was working part-time—estate planning—for a small Wall Street law firm. She hoped that life had been kind to him, and that perhaps—he should feel no obligation—they might meet for dinner or a drink now that she was once again living in New York City.

And now that I'm a widower? he heard himself ask. But how would she have known, he wondered. And: was he flattering himself to imagine that *this* was her reason for writing. He had written back, and—out of curiosity? guilt? *kindness*?—suggest- ed they meet for lunch.

He had considered The West End Bar, or the V & T Pizzeria—places near Columbia University where they had hung out together when they were students, she in the law school, he in the graduate department of English and Comparative Literature—but had decided instead on a restaurant that had *not* been there when they were living together: Henry's, which was at the corner of Broadway and West 105th Street.

When he saw her enter the restaurant, and when she made her way to his table, where she kissed him lightly—her cheek was warm—and when she stepped back and told him how wonderful it was to see him again, how wonderfully *fit* he looked—he found, to his surprise, that tears were welling in his eyes, and that he was doing what he had been warning himself not to do: remembering the first time he had ever seen her.

It had been Veterans Day, 1967. The air was crisp, the sky blue and cloudless, the crowd of anti-war protestors among whom he stood, animated and happy. Across the street, the people who lined the sidewalk behind police barricades with *their* banners, posters, and flags—in support of the war in Vietnam—seemed equally happy, the chants each side launched into the air little more than friendly cheers for rival football teams.

Margaret was wearing a pale V-neck lavender sweater, a purple paisley scarf knotted loosely around her neck. Her wheat-colored hair, shoulder-length, was, in the autumn sunlight, laced with threads of gold, and she appeared to him to have stepped straight out of a Saks Fifth Avenue advertisement so as to take her place—*out* of place—among those whose fashions seemed, for the most part, to have been purchased from clothing racks in Salvation Army thrift stores.

She seemed the kind of woman—beautiful, cool, poised—who had always had the power to intimidate him: a woman who, he assumed, went to debutante balls with self-assured men who were destined to run Fortune 500 companies, to own yachts, and—always, always—to sweat less than he did. What, he wondered at the time, was a woman like this doing in the front line of anti-war protestors? And what could she ever want with an intense, curly-headed Jewish boy from Brooklyn?

Still, when she turned and looked his way, and when she smiled—a quizzical smile, as in: *We've met before, yes?*—he gained the courage he usually lacked, pushed through the crowd, and made his way to her side. He began talking at once—about the rally, about the weather, about the war, about whatever came to mind—and she responded easily. Her hazel-green eyes, above ruddy high-colored cheeks, had seemed almost translucent, and—what he had not expected—warm and inviting.

When she asked his name, then pointed uptown, he saw that a military band was approaching, and that behind the band a phalanx of soldiers in camouflage khakis, rifles to their shoulders, were marching in lock step, motorcycles cruising slowly at their sides. "I'm glad to meet you, Paul," she said, shaking his hand, "but would you excuse me, please?" Then she had turned away, slipped under a wooden baricade, walked out onto Fifth Avenue, and, along with about two dozen others, sat down in the middle of the street, directly in the path of the oncoming parade.

Within a minute, police were there, confiscating the banner she and the others had unfurled—END THE WAR NOW! BRING OUR BOYS HOME!—and dragging them away. It was only when he saw her being led to a police van—she did not, like most of the protestors, trained, he assumed, in passive resistance, go limp, but instead, her hand in the hand of a tall, young policeman, walked up three steps and into the van as if she were being helped into a hansom cab—that it occurred to him that he had not asked her name.

So he found out which station house the protestors were being taken to, and after that, which court house for arraignment, and at seven-thirty that night, when she was released on her own recognizance pending a hearing, he was waiting for her.

"I was hoping you'd be here," she said. She took the single yellow rose he held out to her, inhaled its fragrance, kissed him on the cheek. "Are you hungry?" she asked. "I'm positively ravenous!"

She took his hand in hers, and while she told him about what had happened in the half-dozen hours since her arrest—the judge, she suspected, from his manner, was as opposed to the war as they were; the policeman who put her in the van had asked for her phone number—they made their way to China-town, where they ate and talked, and then talked more, on and on and on. He had walked her home—she lived in Greenwich Village, in a one-bedroom apartment above an Italian restaurant, a few doors down from the Waverly Theater—where she invited him in, and where they made love until dawn. Two weeks later, he moved out of his one-room Upper West Side fifth floor walk-up and into her apartment. They had stayed together for the next three and a half years.

"I trust my letter, coming out of the blue—and with the check—" she began.

"And with the check," he repeated.

"You noticed." She reached across the table, took one of his hands in both of hers. "I trust it didn't shock you, Paul, but I'd been thinking of doing this for so many years that it seemed as if—"

She stopped.

"—as if it would allow you to put the experience to rest?"

"No," she said. "I'd been thinking of sending it for so many years that it seemed as if I'd *already* sent it."

"'Closure,'" he said, "'Closure' is the operative word these days, to judge from conversations with my students. They're forever wanting *closure* on their relationships."

"Closure?" She cocked her head to the side. "Possibly. But as soon as I mailed the letter, I realized the obvious—that what I wanted resembled overture much more than closure."

"Well, here we are," he said. "So that some wishes, it seems—even when unacknowledged—do come true."

"The unconscious never sleeps," she said.

"A good, if sometimes troubling fact," he said. "But I can't accept the check," he added quickly. "In fact, I've already torn it up."

"You shouldn't have."

"For starters, I remember giving you three hundred fifty dollars in small bills to give to the doctor. The check you wrote was for more than twenty-five hundred dollars."

"For starters—" she glanced at a waiter who was standing beside their table "—for starters, I'll have a dry Martini, two olives, no twist."

"The same," Paul said.

She smiled easily, leaned toward him. "I remember the first time I ordered a dry Martini, and you told me that E. B. White claimed it was the only American invention as perfect as the sonnet."

"That was H. L. Mencken," Paul said. "White called it 'the elixir of quietude.'"

She sat up straight. "The amount," she stated, "represented interest on three hundred and fifty dollars compounded quarterly at five percent for forty-one years."

"That's ridiculous, and you know it," he said.

"But it served to compound your guilt enough for you to agree to meet with me."

"It wasn't the check that brought me here," he said. "As far as I can tell, I feel no guilt now, and never did."

"*None?*"

"I've always thought that what we did—what you went through—set us *both* free," he said, and, having anticipated her reaction to his having torn up the check, he continued to speak words he had prepared in advance: "I felt for your pain, of course, if that's the right word—for the *ordeal* you endured, which was surely unpleasant, and, as I recall, made you feel dirty and ashamed—"

"'Sinful' would be the apt word," she interjected, "given that until the age of eighteen, I was taught by nuns."

"Sinful then," Paul said. "And there were all the lies and secrecy, the man asking for a kiss when it was over…"

"Well, some things are better now than they were then. Young people have more options these days, wouldn't you say? They don't have to sneak around the way we did."

"Still bitter, aren't you? I never *insisted*, you know. I—"

"Bitter? Not at all," she said. "Actually, it pleases me that you remember details—the amount, the doctor's gentle perversity—you reacted with such cold logic at the time—such *rationality*—that—"

"Opinions to the contrary notwithstanding, I was not unfeeling, then or now. What was our alternative? To bring an unwanted child into the world who would have been resented, and who—"

Confused momentarily to hear himself rehearsing old arguments, he stopped.

"We don't know that," she said. "When it comes to such matters, we have no double-blind study. As you were fond of saying, we're not living in a first draft. This—our lives now—is it, yes?"

She paused, but he said nothing.

"For my part," she continued, "I think I would have loved the child, and you would have too. It's what I believed at the time, though I lacked the courage to say so—and I believed we might have been happy together. Who knows?"

"Nobody."

Their drinks came, and she raised her glass. "To us," she said.

They drank, looked at their menus, ordered lunch—crab cakes for her, grilled seafood salad for him. They talked easily while they ate, telling each other about the years between, and about their apartments, their jobs, their children. He was in semi-retirement, teaching one seminar a semester, but—the good news—would be permitted to remain in his faculty apartment on Claremont Avenue for the rest of his life; she had bought a two-bedroom co-op on Fifth Avenue at Sixty-Ninth Street, and was working three days a week for Quinn and Janovsky, whose senior partners were men with whom she'd gone to law school. His son and daughter, both married, lived in Brooklyn, and each had two children. All three of her children—two girls and a boy—lived in and around Weston, Connecticut, near to where they had grown up.

Few things in life made her happier than to know that her children were close, she said, and not just geographically. They actually *liked* one another, and this allowed her to believe that perhaps she had gotten a *few* things right in this life. When she said this, her eyes became moist, and she looked away quickly, remarking on how lovely the restaurant was—the arts-and-crafts style design, the soft amber lighting, and—rare thing in New York—the generous space between tables that allowed them to carry on a conversation without having to shout.

He said that Henry's had become a favorite. In fact, it had inspired him to think of working up a *Zagat*-style guide to the fifty *quietest* restaurants in New York City.

"Ah," she said, "but once you published the guide, things would change—"

"You've just given me time for other projects. Thanks."

"Ever the helpmate," she said. "But you *do* have more time now, don't you, Paul? I mean—how be decorous?—I mean, since your wife died."

"Yes."

"Was she ill for a long time?"

"Yes."

"Do you mind my asking, given that—?"

"There's no need to be discreet—that's what you meant, I think—not decorous—but I have no problem talking about

Lorraine. She had an especially debilitating form of MS—her mind was alert to the end, though she did require a good deal of *physical* assistance the last few years, especially with her ADL's."

"ADL's?"

"Activities of Daily Living."

"Like your brother then."

"Like my brother."

"Surely that thought—the parallel, which you could not have wished for—"

"As you noted, the unconscious never sleeps," he said.

"Oh come on, Paul—no need to be snide. Surely it must have crossed your mind that here you were again, being the eternal caretaker..."

"My brother had muscular dystrophy—Duchenne's muscular dystrophy, to be exact, not multiple sclerosis—and yes, the thought crossed my mind, as it did Lorraine's. Taking care of Mort when I was a boy turned out to be excellent preparation for events of recent years. But how did you know?"

"Know you'd made the connection about caring for your wife the way you'd cared for your brother?"

"Know that I was a widower."

"Ah *that*!" she said, and smiled. "I read it in the alumni magazine. My husband, Roger, went to Columbia too, if you recall, and I saw an item in the 'Class Notes—'" She paused, and when he said nothing, continued: "It's how I've followed you through the years—your family, your career. You've become quite the literary critic. I loved your book on the Irish and the Jews, by the way, and—"

"That was a scholarly book, not literary criticism, except in passing—more about immigration patterns and how—"

"—our distinctive cultures influenced the different ways we adapted to our lives in the New World. Do I have it right?"

"You really did read me then."

"My genteel way of stalking, I suppose," she said. "But we

used to talk about this stuff *all* the time. About how *different* our lives were, even though, as it turned out, we'd both been born and raised in Brooklyn, a few blocks from each other. Don't you remember how we used to speculate on our commonalities and differences in the way you do in your book, only much more articulately than I ever could—"

"Back then we were speculating in first draft," he offered, "while in my book I was being articulate through nine years of revisions."

"Sometimes—" she said, and hesitated before going on "—sometimes I like to think that if you hadn't known me, you would never have written the books you've written."

"Sounds about right," he said.

"So that, as you point out, the Irish, like my father, moved into politics, while the Jews, like…" She paused. "Sorry. I can't find the right words, but what I've really been wanting to say, as I tried to do in my note, is that your gift for words used to intimidate me—to make me feel *stupid* somehow. Did you know that? I always felt—*feared*—you were about to *correct* me, and, therefore, of course, to have reason to reject me."

"But you rejected me."

"Only in the fact," she said, "But where was I—? Oh yes— the Irish moved into politics, while the Jews, like—"

"—like me?"

"Like you, yes."

"While the Jews moved into matters more ethereal and intellectual?"

"Yet you were merchants too."

"True, though when it came to my books, not very good merchants."

He looked around the restaurant and, recognizing several colleagues, wondered what they would think, seeing him here with an unfamiliar and attractive older woman. *Your beauty used to intimidate me*, he thought of saying, even though back then—

could he tell her this now?—he had been disappointed to discover she was not upper class WASP, and not even lace curtain Irish like Grace Kelly, but working class Irish. He finished his drink, signalled to the waiter to bring two more.

"To have read T*he Irish and the Jews Come to America*," he said, "is to make you one of a small but quite distinguished elite."

"Oh come on, Paul, you're being—rare thing—falsely modest. You've produced an impressive body of work. Surely you've—"

"No," he said. "I'm being honest. People outside of academia have vastly inflated notions of our successes. Mostly, as I tell my grad students, we're like caretakers in cemeteries, each of us tending to small plots of land—to the graves of one or two dead writers—pulling up weeds, repairing a headstone now and then, chasing away vandals—"

"Why do I get the feeling you're correcting me again?" she asked. "But okay, your book on James—*The Irish Henry James*—surely that attracted an audience beyond academia."

"What did Roger do?"

"Roger was an accountant—well, more than an accountant: he was Chief Financial Officer and Vice President of a paper manufacturing company. You changed the subject."

Their second Martinis arrived, and Paul raised his glass. "To us," he said.

"Maybe it's the alcohol—despite my fabled heritage, I never could hold it well." She grinned. "But okay, okay. I'm feeling fine—quite fine actually, though it saddens me to see you looking so gloomy. Moving right along then, let me be direct: Do you think we can be friends again?"

"Why not?" he said. "The students these days have a category they call friends-with-benefits."

"Which means?"

"What do you think it means?"

She leaned back, a puzzled look on her face. Then her eyes went wide.

"*Really?*" she exclaimed.

"They seem, at least in conversations with me, to have no difficulties with it: with being friends with various people with whom they occasionally sleep. And yet—"

"Forgive me," she said, the back of her hand to her cheek, "but I think I'm blushing, and that this is what Craig, my eldest, would call 'a generation thing.'"

"I was just teasing," he said.

"No you weren't." She looked at him with large, watery eyes.

"Have it your way. I *wasn't* teasing. You *are* still a most attractive woman, Margaret. In fact, when you walked in before, I thought: God—she looks just like her mother did, and your mother was a real looker—movie star gorgeous like the aging stars of the thirties and forties we loved—Irene Dunne, Jean Arthur, Mary Astor—you look the way she did, especially now that you've let your hair go to white—"

"*Silver,*" Margaret corrected. "Mother always insisted that her hair was neither gray nor white, but *silver.* Thank you for the compliment, I suppose—my Martinis and I thank you. What you see is real, by the way—no surgical enhancements. Mother is gone, of course. Yours?"

"Gone."

"Mort?"

"The same—many years ago, and you know what?" he said, unable to keep his voice from rising. "My mother was right when she bolted from the Muscular Dystrophy Association—from all that Jerry Lewis bleed-with-me stuff. Remember how she'd refuse to watch the telethons?"

"I liked your mother. You get your passion from her—especially against injustice—and your eyes: those incredible gray-green-hazel-brown eyes that never stop changing. They're extraordinary. Can we have another round of drinks, do you think?"

"It's been more than half a century, and billions of dollars wasted on research, and in the meantime, no help for the living, for the families that have to cope day by day, and—"

"Care not cure," you used to preach. "I remember you talking about writing a book with that title."

"Did I?"

He motioned to the waiter to take away their plates.

"I'll have coffee," Margaret said to the waiter. Then, to Paul: "Forget the drink, but we do have time for coffee, yes?"

"Oh yes. Lots of time. Being a professor, as Saul Bellow used to say, is a racket."

"Thinking about Mort upset you. I'm sorry. I forgot how close you two were."

"Did you?" Paul asked. He waited, but Margaret stared at him without expression. "He was twenty-nine when he died, and, unlike his brother, without a bitter bone in his body." He forced a smile. "Sorry I got so edgy, but being with you again, well—the memories do find their way home."

"That's a good thing, Paul."

"Why?"

"Because—remember what you taught me, from Cather—Willa Cather—that sometimes memories are—how did it go?—that sometimes memories are better than anything that can ever happen to us again?" She shook her head sideways. "Amazing that she thought that way—and she wasn't even Irish."

"After you and I split, my mother started an organization to help children with muscular dystrophy—take them to ballgames, movies, museums, parks—I drove the van during the summers, and we'd have raffles and Bingo nights to raise money for the outings, and to help families with—"

"—their ADL's?"

"—with their ADL's," he said. "Yes. Thank you. But the organization died when she did."

Margaret started to giggle, covered her mouth. "I got the answer right, didn't I?" she said.

"The answer?"

"To my question."

"I don't understand," Paul said. "You're being too obscure—or too clever—for me, but what I was thinking—what I was about to say—was that I used to want to kill Mort, did I ever tell you that?"

"Yes," she said quietly.

"All the parents—the mothers especially—always saying how *wonderful* their children were, how much they *loved* them, how *blessed* they were, when these kids made their lives into living hells. In our hearts, we were all murderers. You ever have to clean up a two hundred fifty pound sack of a disabled man with a bad case of diarrhea?"

"Not yet."

"Not *yet*? But—" He shook his head sideways, as if to clear it of extraneous matter. "But tell me this," he said. "Besides the work you do with the law firm, and keeping tabs on old flames—what, as people put it these days, what are some of the—awful phrase—*fun things* you do?"

"Ah," she said. "I was hoping you'd ask."

"I'm sorry," he said, and raised his hands in a gesture of surrender. "Really. I'm surprised talking about Mort got to me the way it did."

"I'm not," she said, "but here's the deal, since you ask. I've been on several of their cruises—the ones the alumni association sponsors. I've been to the Galapagos Islands, and on a trip that went from Patagonia to South Africa."

"I get the brochures," he said.

"Have you ever considered going on one?"

"Not yet."

"I tried some of the more exclusive dating services first, and some online sites, and discovered what most women of a certain age discover," she said. "And then a friend of mine from Weston, also a widow, met a man on a cruise—she said she figured out that on a cruise you had a better than average shot at meeting a man of a certain age who was well-educated, had money *and* a curious mind, and, if alone on a cruise, would be in search of a companion."

"So why," he asked, "are you telling me all this?"

"You're teasing again, right?"

"What I think," he said, "is that you were right before—that some things are better now because, as you put it, young people have—dread word—more *options*. But what we had in our years, I've always thought, was something they don't have now—the sense that anything was possible, whether in matters political *or* personal."

She folded her napkin, placed it on the table. "Did you really *always* think that?" she asked.

"Now look—"

"I had this idea for a cartoon a while back, where you see people hustling toward two lines in which men and women are seated at tables across from one another, and above one set of tables there's a sign that says, 'Speed Dating,' and above the other set it says, 'Speed Eating.'"

"That's funny," Paul said. "That's actually very funny."

"I waited seven months after your wife's passing, but it seems that you are, to put a kind spin on things, going to be sitting *shiva* for a very long time."

"Excuse me?"

"You have no intention of ever calling me or seeing me again, do you?"

"I don't understand why you have to—"

"Can you answer the question, please?"

Paul shrugged, but said nothing.

"You knew that when you responded to my note and agreed to meet with me, didn't you?" Margaret stood, steadied herself against the back of her chair with one hand. "I believe our accounts are even. Still, I've decided to let you pay the check today."

She moved to his side of the table, bent down, and, holding to his tie with a firm downward grip, whispered in his ear: "Isn't it amazing what the imagination can do to us? Given your line of work, you should be the expert on that, but really—don't you think it's amazing to realize, after all these years, that I'm not the woman you imagined I was once upon a time, or, for sure, the woman you imagine I am now?"

She kissed him on the cheek, then bit down on his ear lobe. "I had a swell time," she said, and before he could respond, and while he touched his ear with his napkin, hoping, he realized, he might find pinpricks of blood on it, she turned and walked from the restaurant.

Summer Afternoon

Allan Blum and his wife Esther, vacationing in the South of France for the month of December with their friend Sam Gewirtz—in Spéracèdes, a village near Grasse, in the Maritime Alps—stood on the road that led from the church to the cemetery, waiting for the funeral cortege. Two helicopters hovered in the air above them. Behind metal barricades, crowds three and four deep lined both sides of the road, and policemen, in pairs and on horseback, were stationed along the route. Church bells had been ringing steadily.

The sky was dark, without sun or the imminence of sun. The temperature was near freezing—the radio had predicted thunderstorms—and on terraces that rose toward Cabris, a *village perché* a mile or so above Spéracèdes, the undersides of leaves on olive trees appeared in the light breeze to have been brushed with silver.

Late afternoon the day before, on their way back from Nice, where they had had a leisurely lunch and toured the old Russian and Jewish parts of the city, they had been stopped at four separate police check points. They were asked to get out of their car, had their passports and driver's licenses examined, and had been questioned rigorously: What was their purpose in being in France? Why had they rented a house in Spéracèdes, and how long did they intend to stay there? Were they acquainted with the Algerian woman who was accused of murdering the village doctor's wife and child, or with other Algerians who lived or worked in Spéracèdes? Did they employ any Algerians to do housekeeping or gardening...?

Allan and Sam, both in their late sixties, lived near each other on Manhattan's Upper West Side, had grown up in the same Brooklyn neighborhood, and had gone through elementary school, high school, and college together. Five months earlier, Sam had lost his wife Pauline to breast cancer, and when six weeks after this, at the time of the Jewish New Year, Allan suggested Sam join him and Esther for their vacation in France, Sam had agreed at once.

Sam pointed to the far side of the road—to the Hotel Soleillade, where police sharpshooters, in flak jackets, were positioned on the roof and in some of the upper-story windows. "When I lived in Paris for a while, and this was a long, long time ago, before Pauline and I were married," he said, "I remember looking out my window—I had a second-floor apartment on the Boulevard Raspail—and seeing a funeral come by—a large black hearse, and mourners in top hats, and a brass band playing Beethoven's Fifth Symphony."

The church bells had stopped ringing, and police on motorcycles now cruised by slowly, along with journalists, photographers, and television crews. They were followed by four policemen on horseback, then by a phalanx of several dozen police marching in lock-step. Behind them came two teams of horses, one following the other, each team pulling a coffin—a large coffin first, a smaller one second—each coffin covered with a garland of braided red and white flowers.

"The French are really good at this," Sam whispered. "They're terrible at many things, but when it comes to ceremony, they're terrific."

Behind the police, at a distance of some fifteen to twenty yards, a crowd of mourners now appeared. From newspaper and television images, Allan recognized the man in the middle of the front line, a tri-colored sash across his chest, as Doctor Henri Bertrand. Hatless, and wearing a gray three-piece suit— Allan gauged him to be in his early- to mid-forties—the doctor was strikingly handsome in the manner of an Italian movie star, with wavy, graying hair, deep set eyes, and a square chin. His arms were linked with the arms of two elderly women, one to each side of him, and the elderly woman to his right had her arm linked in the arm of a much older woman who walked with difficulty, dragging her left leg slightly. Doctor Bertrand stared straight ahead, and from the proud way he carried himself, he might, Allan thought, have been a hero returning to his home-town in order to witness a statue being unveiled in his honor.

A boy, perhaps five or six years old, in suit and tie identical to Doctor Bertrand's—his surviving child, Allan assumed—walked several feet to his left, hand in hand with a middle-aged woman. A priest, in long black robe, walked to Doctor Bertrand's right, and in the line of people immediately behind Doctor Bertrand walked four other priests, along with three women in brown and white habits, this group followed by a group of two to three dozen others, the women in dresses and topcoats, the men in suits, some of the women pushing baby carriages. Despite the chill in the air, Allan noticed, none of the men wore coats.

On television, the evening before, they had learned the news: that Doctor Bertrand's wife and three-month-old daughter had been found dead in their home, and that the police had taken the family's Algerian housekeeper into custody and would be charging her with the murders.

"Summer afternoon," Esther said.

"*Summer?*" Allan said. "But it's December. I don't understand—"

"Summer afternoon," Esther repeated. "Henry James thought those were the two most beautiful words in the English language."

Stepping out from behind the barricades, people now moved

onto the road to join the funeral procession. Allan turned to Esther and opened his mouth to speak—to ask how she could, in such a moment, be thinking such a thought—but as he did, something caught in his chest and he found himself doubled over, gasping for breath. He could hear Esther, a retired New York City high school English teacher, talking to Sam about Henry James, saying that there was not, as far as she could recall, a funeral anywhere in James's novels or stories. The same was true of Jane Austen. Nor were there any references she could remember in either writer's work to war. And yet, she was saying, *everything* was there—everything that mattered.

"I'm sorry," Allan said. "I didn't want…"

He sat on a bench, Esther on one side of him, Sam on the other, Sam telling him that the same thing had happened to him once, at the funeral of an old girlfriend. Allan's heart began to slow down, to beat more regularly, and he told himself that in a week or so he would visit Doctor Bertrand in his office and have him listen to his heart, and perhaps the doctor's laying on of hands would provide the pretext for conversation. Although the doctor would hardly be a stranger to death, he might now be experiencing a more acute sense of loss than any he had previously imagined possible. The doctor might not want to burden friends and family with his situation, and it might, Allan thought, give the doctor's heart some ease to be able to talk with a stranger—with someone he *didn't* know…

The speaker, on a platform in front of the village's school, was talking about the National Front's *mission civilatrice*, and how the two great dangers facing France were unemployment and immigration. Three million unemployed Frenchmen, he declared, were three million immigrants too many. What had happened in Spéracèdes would soon be happening not only in Paris, Marseilles, or Lyon, but in every village where good and honest Frenchmen and Frenchwomen lived. North Africans and others from that continent were draining France of its resources, and undermining the integrity of French national identity.

The French nation grieved with Doctor Bertrand and his family. Of course. In such a dark time, however, there *was* hope and there *was* light, for the National Front had solutions to France's problems: repatriate these immigrants, restrict their access to French citizenship, create and deploy a special National Guard to prevent civic unrest and subversion...

Allan saw that some of the people applauding most enthusiastically were villagers with whom he exchanged friendly greetings when he walked to and from town. The speaker—not Le Pen, who had sent his regrets and who, since Sarkozy's ascendancy, was limiting his public appearances—was listing items on the National Front's agenda: reintroducing the death penalty, criminalizing abortion, blocking France from further integration with Europe, encouraging French women—their patriotic duty—to have more children. Allan pointed to one of the placards: *Pour le SIDA—SIDAtoriums*.

"Does that mean what I think it does?" he asked Sam.

"Sure does," Sam said. "According to these clowns, people with AIDS are to be placed in special camps."

"Even if they're Jews?" Allan asked.

"Despite my wishful musings, irony won't be selling well here today, I'm afraid," Esther said. "We should leave. I'm feeling distinctly uncomfortable—sick to my stomach actually."

His voice low, Sam was explaining that many of the founders of the National Front had been members of the Nazi Waffen-SS and of terrorist OAS Algerian settlers organizations. Did Allan and Esther know that Le Pen had called the gas chambers a minor footnote in the history of World War Two? Allan looked around, at other slogans on other placards: *La France et les Français D'Abord... La France pour les Français de Souche... Non à l'Islamisation...*

Although the three of them, with Pauline, had, during the

Vietnam War, marched in anti-war protests together, Sam had, with the years, become more politically conservative, and unashamedly so. During the sixties he had been arrested several times during anti-war protests—for sitting in at induction centers, for advocating draft resistance—and in his new political incarnation he had taken to using this fact to chastise Allan—to remind him that for all his ideals and beliefs, Allan had never put his body where his mouth was.

To Allan's surprise and pleasure, however, Sam had within the past year, become a critic of America's wars in Iraq and Afghanistan. Although Sam continued to believe that the United States had a moral and political obligation to use its global hegemony for good, his verdict on these wars was that they were carelessly conceived, badly executed, and, for the most part, politically counter-productive. Still, he maintained, when it came to Iraq, there *was* something to be said for getting rid of at least one brutal dictator, and for letting the Arabs know that if they messed with Israel, the United States would bomb the crap out of them.

When at dinner, their third evening in Spéracèdes, Esther mentioned the fact that on the first day of the American invasion of Iraq, Allan had sent a letter of protest to the White House in which he declared that the war was not being waged in his name, Sam had scoffed, and said this proved one of his major points—not about Allan so much, whose *sincerity* he didn't question, but about liberals in general, and their lack of realism—the *softness* of their views.

Not to speak ill of the dead, he had added, but his wife, Pauline, bless her sweet bleeding heart, had done the same thing—had often written letters to the president expressing her *displeasure* with American policies.

"Puerile," Sam said. "I told her that such acts—letters to the president, or to newspapers or congressmen—protest marches, e-mail petitions—these were all puerile acts. I called them—" he paused for effect "—'The Pueriles of Pauline.'" He had tried to laugh then, but had coughed instead, wiped at his eyes. "Sure," he said a moment later. "'The Pueriles of Pauline'—that's what I used to call them…"

A speaker was recounting the story of Joan of Arc, the National Front's patron saint, who had martyred herself to prevent British domination of France. The speaker talked of ways ethnic minorities would soon dominate French life, and of how all those who championed them—the Left, the Socialists, the Communists, the trade unionists—intellectuals, feminists, homosexuals—were contributing to the degeneration of the nation.

"Are you coming?" Esther asked.

"Not just yet," Allan said.

"I'll meet you back at the house then. Sam—?"

Monsieur and Madame Merle, who owned one of the village's two grocery stores, approached. "I am pleased to see you all here today," Monsieur Merle said.

Allan said he had seen Monsieur and Madame Merle walking with the crowd of mourners, and asked if Madame Bertrand and her children were relatives. Monsieur Merle said that yes, Madame Bertrand was—*had been*, he corrected himself—his niece.

Allan and Esther offered their condolences, and Monsieur Merle thanked them, and said that the reason their presence pleased him was because, as Americans, they could now see for themselves the problem that the good people of Spéracèdes, like good people everywhere, were facing in France.

"Intolerance," Allan said. "Yes. It's despicable."

"*Intolerance?*" Monsieur Merle asked. "How intolerance? What we have in common with you Americans—our great and unfortunate bond—is the knowledge of what happens to a society when it refuses to take strong measures to save itself."

"Uh-oh," Sam said.

"I don't understand," Allan said.

"Esther's right," Sam said, a hand on Allan's arm. "Time to head for the exits."

Allan pushed Sam's hand away. "Tell me about what we have in common," he said to Monsieur Merle. "Please."

"I speak, of course, of your Negroes," Monsieur Merle said. "You set them free within your borders more than a century ago, yet you are still paying the price. They defile your wives and daughters, they destroy your cities, they steal your cars—"

"Excuse me," Esther said, and to Allan: "Coming?"

"I want to hear more," Allan said to Monsieur Merle, "because it seems to me that you and I have *nothing* in common. I would, in fact, be ashamed to have *anything* in common with you."

"Are you then—how do you say it in your country—" Monsieur Merle asked "—a lover of niggers?"

In his left hand, Allan held one of the flyers the National Front had been distributing, and, with a backhanded swing, he lashed out at Monsieur Merle, but Monsieur Merle, a stout man who stood at perhaps five-foot-four, jerked his head back with surprising quickness so that the paper fluttered past his nose.

"You are not French, sir," Monsieur Merle stated calmly. "If you were, you would understand what we live with here. I admire you greatly, you know—you Americans. In Indochina first, and again in Iraq and Afghanistan, you have been the defenders of the West—of Christian civilization—whereas our leaders…"

"I am, for your information, a Jew," Allan said.

Monsieur Merle made a slight percussive sound—*Pouf!*—across his lips, as if to say: Well then—that explains everything, of course, doesn't it?

"Don't say another word," Sam whispered. "These birds make born-again neo-cons like me look like liberal groupies. Come *on*, Allan—forget the noble sentiments, and let's just get the hell out of here, okay?" Sam took Allan by the arm. "I know what the French can be like, believe me. When they're not self-serving cowards, they can be exceptionally gifted at being really mean."

Allan looked toward the speaker's platform, where a man was

holding forth about the necessity of repealing anti-racist legislation—the so-called *liberticides*—about giving the police more power, about ridding the nation of the scum that was fouling its waters, about the sacredness of the nuclear family…

Allan pulled his arm from Sam's grasp. "*Shame!*" he began shouting. "*Shame…! Shame…! Shame on you! Shame on all of you! Shame…! Shame…! Shame…!*"

Then he felt his arms being wrenched behind him, his head yanked downward, chin to chest. Policemen surrounded him, pushed him forward roughly. A large man, not in uniform, stood in their path. Someone pulled Allan's head back by the hair and when he did, the large man, grinning broadly, said something about Allan's wife, after which he drew back his fist and smashed it into Allan's face. Allan heard something click inside his nose. He tasted salt. He heard Esther scream. He saw Sam, arms flailing, fall and disappear into the crowd. But why, he wondered a moment later, had being called a nigger lover—why had this been capable of triggering his rage? Of what real *use*, far from home, were the words he'd shouted? And—a passing thought—was it easier, he wondered, to be openly enraged, or outraged, *because* he was far from home?

When, later on, they would talk about the incident, he imagined that Sam would probably trace the intensity of Allan's feelings to a time when, as boys, they had revered Jackie Robinson—had taken pride in the fact that Robinson played for their home team, the Brooklyn Dodgers—to how, like most of their Jewish friends, they had schooled themselves in the ways Robinson, as fierce a competitor as ever existed, had had to curb his ferocity and turn the other cheek in order to make better lives possible for others. But why, he wondered, too, had the old cliché about Americans being *les défenseurs de la civilisation Occidentale et Chrétienne* riled him so? There were a multitude of more pernicious ways in which people with power and access to power exploited others, or murdered, or were complicit in murder…

While people kicked at him, Allan lay on the ground—on one of the village's *boules* courts—curled into a fetal position. Although he had, forty years before, attended many civil rights and anti-war demonstrations, this was the first time he had ever been attacked physically, and—a not unpleasant thought—the first time he had acted so as to cause police to intervene and take him away.

Make-A-Wish

Charlie Teitlebaum, a forty-two-year-old surgeon born and raised in the same Boston neighborhood in which Howard had grown up, had not been one of Howard's residents, but while Charlie was doing his internship at The George Washington School of Medicine, where Howard was on the faculty, Howard and Charlie had become friends. At the time, Charlie had been going through a difficult stretch—his wife, Caitlin, had, it turned out, been in and out of mental hospitals during her late teens and early twenties (Charlie only learned this *after* they were married), and, following their move to Washington, had begun throwing tantrums during which she would physically attack him.

When, during rounds one morning, Howard noticed how uncharacteristically distracted Charlie seemed, he suggested that Charlie come see him, and when Charlie did, and Howard asked the obvious question—*Is everything okay?*—Charlie had begun talking, and had kept on talking for the next two hours.

Howard met with Charlie regularly for several weeks, and during their talks he repeated what he saw as the essential questions: If you stay with her, will you be able to finish your internship? Can you see yourself living with her for the rest of your life? And: If you think her life will continue to go down the tubes, why the duty—the *need*—to join in her descent?

Seven months later, Charlie divorced Caitlin, and eighteen months after that—and after a brief romance with Deirdre, who was one of Howard's residents at the time—Charlie remarried.

Charlie's second wife, Claire, was a pediatrician, and by the time Charlie had completed a six year residency in general surgery at Johns Hopkins, followed by a two year fellowship in surgical oncology, they had had three children. By this time, too, Charlie owed the Army a dozen years of service.

In 1999 Charlie was assigned to Walter Reed Army Medical Center in Washington, D.C., where he distinguished himself in general and oncological surgery. In October, 2001, less than a month after the attacks on the World Trade Center, he was sent to Afghanistan with a medical team that accompanied the first troops landing there.

Following a year-long tour in Afghanistan, he returned to Walter Reed, and four years later was deployed to Iraq. In Iraq, he reported in a letter to Howard, his Forward Surgical Team traveled more than twelve hundred miles within four months of its arrival. Medical teams had been designed and trained for swift, mobile military operations, but the war in Iraq was proving to be slow-moving and protracted; blast injuries from suicide bombs and land mines brought about higher incidences of penetrating wounds, mangled extremities, and blindness. Charlie saw astonishing rates of pulmonary embolism and deep venous thrombosis, and, what alarmed him most, a near epidemic of multi-drug resistant *Acinetobacter baumannii* infection.

Two weeks before Howard received Deirdre's letter, telling him of *her* situation, and asking him if he would do what they were now doing—travel with her in France for ten days—he had received a letter from Charlie's wife Claire. Three days prior to Charlie's scheduled departure from Iraq, Claire wrote, while making his weekly telephone call home from outside his barracks, he had been hit during a rocket-propelled grenade attack.

Despite the Forward Surgical Team's best efforts, Howard now told Deirdre, they had been unable to revive him.

"So that means that later this year, Charlie and I will be having a mini-reunion," Deirdre said.

"Don't," Howard said.

"Why not?" She jabbed Howard in the side, and when he winced, she did it again. "Come on—why *not*?"

They were traveling west on the autoroute and were, Howard estimated, about a half hour from Aix-en-Provence. They planned to stop for lunch in Aix before going on to Saint Rémy, where Howard's daughter Julia, a student at Tufts, was spending part of her junior year abroad. The fact that Julia was in France, Charlie had told himself, and that there was an international conference on infectious disease taking place that week not far from Saint Rémy—in Montpellier—would make his time with Deirdre—the logistics and the alibis—easier.

"The way I see it, Charlie was just doing his job—being responsible the way you taught us," Deirdre said. "What do they call it in bioethics—his deontologic obligation, right?—that if called upon to heal, you have to say yes because you may be the only one capable of performing that particular mission of healing. Charlie was a good guy. He was smart and cute—and shy, I remember—like you."

"Shy?"

"Well, in that category, you did overcompensate prodigiously," she said. "But I'll bet, where he is now, he's changed, and that, emulating his mentor, he no longer considers himself bound by marital vows."

"How can you be sure?"

"Because I know what men are like," she said, and slipped her hand under Howard's shirt.

Howard pushed at her hand. "Come on. I'm driving and—"

"And what? You'll crash and kill us? Hey—that way Charlie and I will get to be together even sooner—or—hmmm—perhaps the three of us…"

"A heavenly *ménage à trois*?"

"Sounds good to me." She rested her head on Howard's shoulder. "It's only my hands and feet that have been turning numb lately—not my brain. And this *is* an historic occasion, you know—the trip you and I used to fantasize about, even though you were married back then too."

"I'm sorry. I—"

"Shh," Deirdre said, cutting him off. "No need." She laughed. "I remember the first time we had a drink together after work— we were flirting outrageously, and I asked you about your marriage—forward then, too, I was—and you said you believed in marriage but that you weren't a fanatic about it." Deirdre laughed again, then coughed. "Ouch."

"'Ouch' for the memory?"

"No. For cramps."

What Deirdre had written in her letter to Howard was that she had been diagnosed with ovarian cancer, and that after a debulking—didn't he love the word?—chemotherapy, and first-, second-, and third-line drugs, her doctors didn't have much left to offer her. So she had contacted the Make-A-Wish Foundation, which enabled children with life-threatening medical conditions to have dream vacations, or to spend time with their favorite athletes, movie stars, or rock groups. The sad news, however, was that they did not yet have a program for adults. Therefore, because Howard was the kindest man she'd ever known, and because she was in dire need of a huge dose of his tenderness, she had decided it was time to collect on the promise he had made to her once upon a time.

Howard saw that, arms extended, palms against the dashboard, Deirdre was now bracing herself, squeezing her eyes shut.

"Hey—are you okay?" he asked.

"I am, but my stomach's not. We'd better stop."

Howard drove the car onto the shoulder of the highway. Deirdre got out quickly, leaned on the front fender.

"I should have warned you before," she said, "but I thought the cramping—it's become violent—would pass."

Then she was vomiting profusely—the stuff shooting out of

her mouth and onto the road, some of it splashing onto her shoes. Howard put his arm around her, rubbed the back of her neck.

"Oh shit," she said, looking down. "And I mean it literally—some of it may already be fecal material I'm vomiting, Howard. *Fuck*—!

"Let's get you to a hospital."

Deirdre wiped her mouth with the back of her hand. "There's blockage, right, doc?" she said. "An intestinal obstruction would be *my* diagnosis. When the stuff wants to go down and out the back way but can't, it decides to reverse direction and go back up, right?"

Howard took a bottle of water from the car, wet his handkerchief, started to clean Deirdre's face. She snatched the handkerchief from him, wiped off her mouth and chin, blew her nose, then poured water onto her shoes, swiped at them.

"Damn," she said. "I didn't want you to see me like this."

Howard helped her back into the car, tapped on her abdomen—she didn't resist—and heard what he didn't want to hear: a sound like that coming from a hollow drum.

"Distended as hell," Deirdre said. She sucked air, then sipped water. "Dehydration—another promising symptom. It's great to be a physician at a time like this, don't you think? Nice to really *know* something for a change—to be able to predict the future with a not unreasonable chance of being right."

Howard drove back onto the highway, pressed on the accelerator until the speedometer showed that the car was moving at a hundred and twenty kilometers an hour.

"Headaches lately too," Deirdre said. "Thought I'd mention them. Listen to the patient and the patient will give you the diagnosis—isn't that what we were taught? Really *nasty* headaches the last few nights, and damn!—I'm messing up your plans, the time you wanted to spend with your daughter, aren't I?"

"There's a hospital in Aix," Howard said. "We can stop there. In the meantime—"

"Forget Aix," Deirdre said. "I was this way in the States, and with decent intervals between sieges. Well, it *passed*, right? So, based on *past* experience—hey, doc, I got off a good one—I should be okay for the next two to three hours. That means we can get to Saint Rémy, get me to a doctor there—"

"To a hospital."

"Okay. Have it your way—to a hospital—but in Saint Rémy, please, because if I have to stay over in Aix, it'll screw up your reunion with Julia, and if it does, we have to think of the toll that would take on *me*."

She opened her window, let Howard's handkerchief fly away.

"Hey!" he said. "If a cop's out there—"

"Then we'll get an escort," she said. She touched his hand. "I'll be okay till Saint Rémy. I promise."

When Deirdre woke, they were driving along an avenue that bypassed the center of Aix-en-Provence. The street was lined on both sides with tall plane trees, their limbs, pruned back severely in early winter, looking, Howard thought, as if they had been amputated.

"Traffic willing, we'll be in Saint Rémy within an hour," Howard said.

"I like it when we do things *my* way," Deirdre said. "You weren't always this accommodating, you know. Only when we get there, I don't want some French jerk shooting me up with a lot of drugs, or shoving things up my butt. The French do that more than we do, I hear."

"The French do like their suppositories," Howard said, and let his right hand rest on her stomach. "We're really doing okay?"

"*We?*" She put her hand on top of his. "I like it when you use that word. But hey—don't be scared. *I'm* not. I'm in pain, for sure, but I'm not scared. Pain is okay. It means I'm still here. So why aren't I scared, you may ask?" She sighed. "Because I'm with the man I love. I mean, what some women won't do to get their guy."

When they arrived at their destination in Saint Rémy, the Villa Glanum, a hotel named for a nearby Roman ruin, Howard brought his suitcase into the reception area. He gave the man at the front desk his name, told him he was a physician, that he had a friend who was ill and that he had to get her to a local hospital as quickly as possible. The man replied that there was no hospital in Saint Rémy—that the nearest hospitals were in either Arles or Avignon, each of which was about a half-hour away.

Howard recognized the name of one of the hospitals in Avignon—Hôpital Henri Duffaut—and asked the man to write down directions and, also, to telephone his daughter—he wrote down her number—and to tell her he would call as soon as he could.

In the center of Avignon, outside the fortress-like walls that contained the Palace of the Popes, traffic was barely moving.

"More blockage?" Deirdre asked, and began to sing: "*Sur le pont d'Avignon. La la la la—la, la la la—la…*"

Howard saw that, eyes shut, Deirdre was biting down hard on her lower lip. As soon as they made their way to an intersection, he took a left turn and drove south for several blocks, then west until he reached a street he thought would lead to the hospital, and when, a few minutes later, he saw signs for the university, he was relieved: the hospital, he recalled, had adjoined the university. Less than a minute later, he spotted the building he was hoping to see—a large red brick structure with green slate mansard roofing.

He pulled up in front and looked for signs directing them to the emergency ward, but found instead a bronze plaque stating that the building, designated as a national monument, housed administrative offices for the University of Avignon.

"Shit!" he exclaimed.

"That's *my* word," Deirdre said.

He rolled down his window, called to several young people,

and asked where the hospital was. They told him there was no hospital here, but that there was one on the other side of the Palace of the Popes, by the river.

"My problem, I decided—one of them, anyway," Deirdre said, "is that I became attached to you at an early and vulnerable age. But consider, too, our friend Charlie, poor guy, who had a thing for Irish women like some other Jewish physicians I've known."

Behind them, cars were honking. Howard pictured Charlie, in a makeshift phone booth, lifting a receiver, smiling in anticipation of talking with his wife and children, of telling them he'd be home in less than a week. Howard looked for a phone booth, saw one about twenty yards away, opened the car door. Had he brought a phone card with him?

He ran toward the booth, heard people shouting at him, then heard the staccato blasts of a whistle. Deirdre was calling to him, pointing to a policeman on a motorbike who was signaling to Howard with a white-gloved hand to return to the car. The policeman, dark-skinned and unsmiling—Algerian? Moroccan?—ordered him to get back into the car and to leave at once.

Howard explained that he was an American physician, that he was looking for Hôpital Henri Duffaut, that the woman with him—also a physician—was ill and needed to be taken to a hospital immediately. The policeman, his visor raised, leaned forward, stared at Deirdre for a moment, nodded, took out his mobile phone, spoke into it and, after informing Howard that Hôpital Henri Duffaut had been relocated to another part of the city more than a dozen years before, gestured to Howard to follow him.

Howard followed the policeman until, at the third intersection, they came to a wide cross street where two police cars were waiting, their flashers swirling. The policeman on the motorbike pointed to the cars and, as sirens began blasting on and off, he waved goodby. Howard followed the police cars.

"I like listening to you speak French," Deirdre said. "I meant to tell you that. Later—there will be a later, right?—will you talk to me in French? And I liked his gloves. For my first communion, I had a beautiful pair of white leather gloves my Aunt Bridget gave me." Deirdre doubled over, tried, without success, to keep from moaning. "God but it hurts, Howard. If this is what labor's like, I'm grateful I never…"

She choked, coughed, shook her head back and forth violently, as if by doing so she could shake the pain from it.

"We're almost there," Howard said, and, hoping to distract her, asked if she had been in love with Charlie.

"Wasn't everybody?"

"He was very handsome—and exceptionally fit, I remember," Howard said. "And when you took up with him, he was just coming out of his marriage. The two of you must have had some good times."

"'Good times' you say—could you clarify your terms, doctor?"

"You know what I mean."

"Did you mean, for example—'Was it good for me too?'"

"Well, you never lacked for passion, and I just…"

"You're jealous," Deirdre said. "My, my. I actually think you're jealous and that's a new one—a guy being jealous of a dead friend. Remarkable, really." She closed her eyes, leaned back, let a rasping, guttural sound rumble from her throat. "Men," she said softly.

When they arrived at the hospital, its façade a flat surface of Mondrian-like squares in yellows, blues, and reds, and turned into the driveway that led to Emergency Services, two men in green hospital garb were waiting on a ramp, a gurney next to them. Howard went to Deirdre's side of the car, where hospital aides were already helping her onto the gurney. Deirdre reached for Howard's hand, asked him not to leave her. He kissed her on the forehead, inhaled the foul residue of her vomiting.

"Come on—you can do better than that," she said.

He leaned down, kissed her on the mouth. Her lips were cold. At the doors that led into the hospital a security guard stopped him. Howard took out his wallet, showed the guard a card that identified him as a medical doctor. A policeman was beside Howard, telling him that he would park Howard's car and bring the keys to the nurse's station in the emergency room. Howard entered the hospital, saw that the staff was already checking Deirdre's vital signs, moving her along. They disappeared behind swinging doors. Howard pushed through, watched two men lift Deirdre and place her on an examining table. They began cutting away her clothes, listening to her chest, attaching wires. They moved quickly, efficiently.

A young man, clipboard in hand—his ID tag identified him as Clément Hémon, M.D.—asked Howard to tell him what happened. Howard began, quickly, to give the doctor Deirdre's history, to tell him about the cramps, the headaches, the pain, the vomiting.

A woman in a white lab coat was probing Deirdre's stomach, asking her questions, in English: Did this hurt? When had she last moved her bowels? How often had she been throwing up?

Doctor Hémon thanked Howard, conferred with the woman in the white lab coat. Howard went toward them but was held back by an aide who told him that Doctor Joussaume— the woman who was examining Deirdre—could speak with him later on if he wished.

Doctor Joussaume took Deirdre's hand in her own. "We're going to take you into surgery as soon as we can," she said. "We'll sedate you. Do you have any allergies? Do you know your blood type? We will test for it, of course, but if…"

Other personnel now entered the room, two of them transferring Deirdre to another gurney, rolling her away. Deirdre waved to Howard, who started toward her, but was held back by another man.

"I'm Doctor Rosenthal," the man said, in English.

Howard spoke in French, as clearly and rapidly as he could, telling the doctor what he had told Doctor Hémon: that he was a physician, that Deirdre had cancer of the ovaries—*cancer des ovaires:* the words were cognates—virtually identical, Howard explained—that she had exhausted all the usual lines of treatment, and that during their drive to Saint Rémy she had begun throwing up fecal matter. Deirdre was a physician, he continued, and had been his student at The George Washington School of Medicine, in Washington, D.C.

Doctor Rosenthal made no attempt to interrupt Howard, and Howard wondered why he couldn't stop talking. What Howard wanted to know—he *would* get to the point, he added apologetically—was if he could be present when they performed the surgery. Doctor Rosenthal said that they had paged Doctor Coursaget, an *excellent* surgeon, who would arrive within a half hour. If Howard wished to attend the surgery, he would of course grant him this courtesy. Howard thanked the doctor and suddenly realized that all the while Doctor Rosenthal was talking to him in English, he had been talking to the doctor in French.

The doctor shook Howard's hand. "Your friend is very sick," he said, "but we will do our best for her."

It had been at least a dozen years since Howard had attended a major surgical procedure and, feeling like a small boy allowed into the world of grown-ups, he watched with fascination as Doctor Coursaget and his assistants opened Deirdre's belly, found the dilated loops of bowel through which nothing—neither liquids nor the gaseous content of her intestine—was flowing, located the tumors that were blocking the intestines, and cut them away.

The music coming from the speakers was slow jazz, a woman—Sarah Vaughn? Dinah Washington?—singing a song Howard thought was called "Dreamy." Doctor Coursaget, humming to the tune, was now removing his gloves and his mask, nodding to an assistant, asking the assistant to finish up.

The assistant gestured to a nurse, who pressed a button, the music changing to something louder, and with a more savage, driving beat: what Howard assumed was called hard rock.

"We did the best we could," Doctor Coursaget said to Howard. "Your friend will need to stay in the hospital for four or five days, and I believe she will, for a while at least, benefit from some alleviation of pain. After that…"

The doctor shrugged, gestured with his hands, palms upturned, in a way that indicated there really was not much that he or anyone else could do for Deirdre.

"It is often quite difficult to close up a woman after this particular surgery," he said. "So, as you can see, I have left the truly demanding work to my younger colleague, Doctor Maubert, in whom I have great confidence. We made a decision not to remove her uterus, by the way—a consideration of the extra time involved and possible post-operative complications. These would be negligible in most instances, but given your friend's condition, if we…"

Howard had stopped listening. He looked around: the operating suite was impeccably modern—as high-tech as any he had ever seen. But why was he surprised? He watched Doctor Maubert bend down over Deirdre's stomach and imagined Charlie stitching up soldiers in a tent in Iraq, and he wondered: If he had known the day would end this way, would he have chosen to tell Deirdre about Charlie? Yet when he had, he realized, she had shown little surprise, and the obvious occurred to him for the first time: that she had already known about Charlie, and that his death was the reason for her decision to write to him.

Doctor Coursaget was telling Howard that either he or Doctor Joussaume would be checking in on Deirdre at least once every day. Howard moved away from the doctor, toward Deirdre. He saw Doctor Maubert reach inside Deirdre's body, after which the room began to go dark, the floor to rise toward him.

"Come with me, please," Doctor Coursaget was saying, his hand gripping Howard's elbow.

Howard wanted to push the man away, but the only thing he could do was stare at the pair of pale gloved hands that were vanishing inside Deirdre's stomach. And if she had known about Charlie—one of the medical students they'd been friends with would surely have given her the news—had she, then, proposed their ten days in France not out of her need to be comforted, but out of consideration for his feelings, so that, after she was gone, by having been able to make good on his promise, he would feel absolved of a measure of his guilt?

He sat on a bench, his head between his legs, and could not recall having walked from the operating room to the corridor in which he was now sitting. Doctor Coursaget sat beside him.

"It happens to all of us," Doctor Coursaget said, a hand on Howard's shoulder. "There is no need to be embarrassed."

Howard sat up, drank from the glass of water Doctor Coursaget offered.

"We did the best we could," Doctor Coursaget said again. "Your friend will be in the recovery room for a while, and you can visit with her there. We sedated her quite heavily, however, so I do not expect that she will wake for several hours."

A few minutes later, the doctor shook Howard's hand and left, and as Howard walked toward the exit—he would retrieve the car keys, then go to the parking lot and get Deirdre's suitcase—he realized that not only had no one asked for payment, or for either of them to fill out forms, but no one had even asked that he or Deirdre show proof of insurance.

He stepped outside, and, momentarily blinded by the bright winter sun, felt as if he had walked straight into a wall of pure white light. He felt dizzy, held onto a railing, realized that if it was Charlie's death that had inspired her to write to him, it was also possible that she had done so—that she had wanted him to be with her now and to see her like this—out of something other than kindness.

Overseas

My father and I sat at the kitchen table, old newspapers stacked high, and he went over maps and photos of the Normandy Invasion with me, explaining how and why we won the war in Europe. I was ten years old. I tried to memorize numbers, and then names of generals: 4000 transports, 800 warships, more than 11,000 aircraft; Eisenhower, Patton, Bradley, Ramsay, Leigh-Mallory, von Rundstedt, Rommel. My father showed me where our forces established beachheads, at the base of the Cotentin Peninsula—Utah Beach and Omaha Beach—and he drew a line where General Bradley's forces cut off the peninsula, forcing the Germans to surrender.

Then he pushed the newspapers aside and went through the day's mail and tore up envelopes. He roughed my hair, put the shredded pieces of envelope in the garbage pail under the sink, and told me he'd heard a funny story at work he was thinking of sending to the "Can You Top This?" radio program. The story was about a man who, while taking his physical exam for the Army, pretended to be blind. Later that day the man went to a movie to celebrate being classified 4F, and found himself sitting next to one of the doctors who'd examined him. "Excuse me," the man said, "but could you tell me if I'm on the right train for Jamaica?"

My father laughed before he finished telling his joke, and while I laughed with him he coughed so hard blood began splattering out of his mouth, and he tried to stop it from staining the newspapers by covering his mouth with a handkerchief. I brought him a glass of water and a fresh handkerchief, and he started to thank me but this only made him cough more. He coughed from where metal had dug out sections of his lungs. Most of the fragments had been removed at a field hospital in Italy, but the doctors told him there were still small pieces of metal they had to leave inside for the time being, and my mother had been after him to go to a Veterans Hospital to have them taken out.

"Always remember to tear up anything with our name on it," he said. "If the garbage collectors spill our garbage into the street, or if dogs and cats do the same, and if a policeman finds a piece of paper with our name on it, we could be fined." He reminded me that this had happened to him once, in the first month after he returned home from the war.

My father went into the bedroom, and when he did my mother came into the kitchen and poured herself a glass of whiskey. "So what are *you* looking at?" she asked.

"Nothing," I said.

"Damned right. A lady can't even take a drink anymore without her own son giving her the evil eye." She reached into her housecoat, took out a Hershey bar and broke off a piece for me. "Come here."

I went to her. "I love you, Willy," she said. "You know that, don't you?"

"Yes."

She peeled back the silver foil liner of the chocolate bar, then kissed each of my eyes, and I imagined that we were both remembering how quiet it used to be at night while my father was overseas and it would be just the two of us sitting at the kitchen table the way we were now, flattening out the candy liners to make baseball-sized hard silver balls from them that I'd bring to the Armory to help the war effort.

By the time I woke the next morning, my father was already

gone, and Uncle Joe was in the bedroom with my mother. They were laughing, and playing Johnny-on-the-Pony and Ringalevio-One-Two-Three. I ate a piece of the coffee cake my father had brought home. He worked as a baker for Ebinger's Bakery, and he said they were good people even though they were Germans. "An American is always an American," he said.

Uncle Joe was a policeman in downtown Brooklyn, where the A & S department store, and the Paramount, Fox, and Albee Theaters were, but before the war he was the cop on our beat, and he and my father had been good friends. I'd played boxball with them in front of our house, and sat with them on our stoop when they listened to baseball games on the radio.

Uncle Joe's holster was on top of the ice box, but he'd taken his gun into the bedroom with him, and I was frightened that if my mother went wild the way she did sometimes, and scratched him, he would whack her with the gun. During the two years my father was in the Army, Uncle Joe had stayed with us most nights.

"Your father's a good man who served his country well," Joe said to me while he strapped his holster back on.

"Why didn't you?"

"Because somebody had to keep the home fires burning, kiddo."

"Anyway, Joe was too old," my mother said.

"He could have lied about his age," I said.

Joe winked at me. "Honesty's the best policy," he said.

"Look who's talking," my mother said, and she poured herself a glass of whiskey.

"Hey, put that bottle away," Joe said. "It's too early."

He tried to grab the bottle, but got my mother's arm instead.

"I can do what I want," she said. "It's a free country, ain't it?"

I saw how deep Joe's fingers were into her arm, so I let out words I'd been holding inside me: "You should have beat up on the Nazis and not on my mother."

"And you mind your own goddamned business!" my mother said, and she pushed Joe away.

"Make me!" I said. "It's a free ccountry, ain't it? You always do what *you* want!"

"Like hell I do," she said, and she slapped me.

"Easy on the boy," Joe said. "Go easy now, sugar. Easy."

"What kind of rotten son am I raising?" my mother said. "Tell me that. What kind of a mouth does the boy have on him, huh?"

I felt a ball of tears rolling up through my throat, but I kept it from reaching my eyes.

"Ah, he's a good boy," Joe said. "He knows how to keep a secret. He knows what's good for him, right?"

After Joe left, my mother tried to make up to me. She kept telling me how sorry she was—how if life was perfect we'd all be angels floating on clouds above the rooftops. She drank her glass of whiskey in one swallow, then walked around the kitchen, the way she did during the war, holding the glass to her cheek and singing the song she used to sing me to sleep with: "*Over there. Over there. We're coming over. We're coming over. And we won't be back till it's over, over there…*"

"Jesus, Willy," she said, when she stopped singing. "What am I gonna do, huh? What am I gonna do?"

I imagined her floating over a trench in Italy, with my father below, shivering, hungry, and covered with mud. I saw her drifting down to him, at night, when all the other soldiers were asleep or dying, and she looked as beautiful as a movie star to me—as if her eyes and mouth were twenty or thirty times their regular size so that you could lie down inside them if you wanted.

That night I heard her explain to my father that he left too early for work, so that when she got out of bed to go to the bathroom or have breakfast with him, she was still groggy and bumped into things. That was where her bruises came from. All she wished was for him to be kind with her the way he used to be. "We can't keep blaming everything on the war, Jake," she said. "After all, we *won* the war, right?"

"Sure," my father said. "We won the war, but like they say, we lost a few battles."

"Yeah," she laughed. "You could say that too, couldn't you?"

She spotted me watching from the foyer. "Hey Willy," she called. "Did you hear what your father said? We won the war but we lost a few battles too. Ain't he got a way with words, our old man?"

She leaned over my father then, while he ate his roll and butter, and when she kissed him on the back of the neck, his head snapped up straight, as if she'd rammed him with one of her knitting needles.

The next morning he did what my mother wanted. He stayed in bed late, and while she took a bath, he came into my room and told me he would never stop loving her, no matter what.

"She kept me alive over there," he said. "Just remembering how she'd take my face in her hands and, her eyes shining, tell me, 'I love you, Jake!'—that was what kept me alive and enabled me to come home and see you both again."

"Over there you were a real hero," I said, "weren't you?"

"No," he said. "Not at all. I did my job and was fortunate to be in the right place at the right time. I was able to kill a few of our enemies, and my fellow soldiers were able to save my life. We're talking about chance, Willy—about minutes and miles. If I'd moved a minute earlier or later. If the bullet had been an inch lower or higher. If the field hospital had been a mile further away. If the doctor had been more fatigued or less skilful. You can take any moment in time and think of all the contingencies, and see how fortunate we are, and thereby come to understand our obligations."

"I don't understand you when you talk like this," I said.

"I think you do, Willy. Tell me: What have I taught you?"

"That I should always tear up envelopes. That an American is always an American. That you'll never stop loving my mother."

"You're the best son a father could wish for, and someday you're going to be a fine man," he said. "For a while you may be the only man in your mother's life, but I have great confidence in you. Here are three dollar bills. You get started now. You take your mother out to breakfast, and see that she has a good meal. Leave a generous tip. It never hurts to be nice to people."

I went into their bedroom and told my mother that father was still at home, but that he'd switched his shift and wouldn't be leaving for a while, and that I wanted to take her out to breakfast.

When she finished brushing her hair dry, she stood in front of the mirror and pinned her maroon felt hat onto the side of her head. Its feather was the golden brown color her hair was in the summer. She said it made her look and feel old to have a son grown up enough to take her out to eat, so I told her how pretty she was, and I repeated jokes I knew, and I tried to act in a way that would make her look younger—the way I imagined she'd looked inside my father's head during those times when she'd been saving his life.

When Uncle Joe came to our apartment that morning and got into bed, my father was waiting in the bedroom. My father shot Uncle Joe, and then he shot himself. When I came home from breakfast, the apartment was quiet. I went into the bedroom first, and then I brought my mother in, to show her what had happened.

The State of Israel

When Ira opened his good eye, the men were still there, staring down at him. Doctor Chehade, who had performed the eye surgery the day before, reached under the sheet and took one of Ira's hands in his own.

"It was as I thought," he said, speaking in English. "Several of your arteries had significant occlusions. In addition, there is evidence of a prior myocardial infarction—a *silent* heart attack, I believe you call such events. Am I correct, Doctor Guérard?"

A lime-green surgical mask dangling around his neck, Doctor Guérard nodded, then spoke to Ira in French. Struggling to comprehend what he was saying—the words came to him as if through heavy gauze—Ira asked the doctor to speak in English.

"Ah yes, well when I saw what was occurring with the occlusions, I did the angioplasties. Three. *Coated* angioplasty—stents, you call them, yes?—so there should be minimal fibrosis—scar tissue from the inflammatory, yes?—and for the rest, I am not worried."

"Why should you be," Ira said. "It's not *your* heart."

"*Je ne comprends pas.*" Doctor Guérard turned to Doctor Chehade. "Did I use the wrong languages?"

Doctor Chehade explained that Ira had been making a joke.

"*Ah—tu rigoles avec moi!*" Doctor Guérard exclaimed. "That shows that your spirit is remaining vital. It is always a good warning when the patient is to joke with the doctor. *Donc.* It was my correct decision to not open your chest to do the *pontages*—the grafts—yes?"

"Where am I?" Ira asked.

Doctor Chehade explained that Ira was lying on a gurney in a hallway until a new room could be assigned to him.

"When can I get out of here?" Ira asked. "Out there—*dehors, là-bas*—people are *dying*—"

"In here too," Doctor Chehade said, and turned to Doctor Guérard, who said that he wanted Ira to stay in the hospital for at least one more night to allow time for the anesthesia to wear off.

"*Then* I can go?"

"Perhaps," Doctor Guérard said, and added that he would visit Ira later in the day to talk with him about a cardiac rehabilitation program, and about "*le stress*"—about Ira's work schedule in the United States.

Ira shifted a lever so that he was in a sitting position on the gurney, and he became aware, for the first time, of a weight on his leg. He lifted the sheet, saw that a sandbag had been placed over his thigh where a catheter had been inserted into the femoral artery. He looked over his shoulder, expecting to see a nurse's station, but saw only a long, dimly lit corridor, the pale glow of television sets coming from rooms on both sides of the hallway, but without sound. Was everybody asleep already? Had they forgotten he was there? Had he died and been transported to some medical purgatory where he would spend eternity waiting in a silent corridor—a world without words—for a bed?

He considered climbing down from the gurney in order to find a nurse, but if he did, he was afraid he might bleed onto the floor, or become dizzy and pass out. *A world without words*: wasn't that what his wife Hannah had named the hours they were able to spend together—hours they cherished—when they took walks together, hand in hand, or when they sat and read, evenings, in their living room, without music or television.

Ira, a pediatrician with a practice in Brooklyn's Park Slope neighborhood, had arrived in France three days earlier, to attend an international medical conference in Nice, and it was at this conference that he had become friendly with Doctor Chehade. Doctor Chehade had inquired about the patch Ira wore over his eye, and Ira had explained that it was the result of being hit in the eye by a tennis ball several weeks before. He and Doctor Chehade talked easily with each other, and Ira quickly learned that the doctor had worked and studied, early in his career, at Hadassah Hospital in Jerusalem, where Ira had also spent time. On two evenings, he and Doctor Chehade had had dinner together—had talked about Hadassah Hospital, about Israel, about their families, their work—and it was to Doctor Chehade's hotel room that Ira had gone at once, earlier in the day, when he experienced sudden tell-tale flashing signs at the periphery of his vision, signs that he knew were symptomatic of the beginnings of retinal detachment.

"Yes, I agree that sleep is of utmost importance at a time like this," the man was saying, "and so I am grateful that you have slept so well. We French, you know, still believe in the *cure de sommeil*, which I understand finds little favor in your country even though it has proven quite effective, especially for women."

Ira was not aware of when this man, dressed in suit and tie, had arrived, or of how long he had been there. The man was explaining that of course one utilized medications—combinations of anti-anxiety and anti-depressant medications, along with *hypnotiques*—but that what was essential to the sleeping cure was that patients be removed from the ordinary anxieties that pressed upon them, that they be put into prolonged states of calm in which they would be cognizant not only of the sanctuary the doctor was providing, but also of the real world that could be perceived, if at a distance, through the veil of sleep and dreams.

"Who are you and why are you telling me this?" Ira asked.

"But I am Doctor Chehade," the man said. "I was waiting for you to awaken so that we might have a conversation before I leave for home. Also, I would like to take a look at your eye again. So come—I will take you to your room."

Doctor Chehade, whose voice had a mellow, liquid quality that Ira found beguiling, reached below the gurney, unlocked the brake, and, holding an IV pole with one hand, pushed Ira along the corridor.

"I was able to obtain a private room for you, which is one reason for the delay," he said. "But also, I wanted to talk with you of something existent on a more personal note."

In the hospital room, Doctor Chehade offered Ira his hand, and when Ira stood in the space between bed and gurney, he felt his knees give way.

"I'm weak," he said. "The journey from the gurney, right?"

Doctor Chehade laughed. "I agree with Doctor Guérard—the fact that your sense of humor has not departed is an excellent indicator of regeneration. But you have not eaten for many hours, and so I have ordered a special dinner for you. I think you will be pleased."

"Thanks." Ira sat on the bed. "You've been very kind."

"It has been my pleasure, for a man of your eminence and generosity." Doctor Chehade smiled. "I took the liberty of searching for you on the internet, you see, and I state now that the honorable charitable work you have done in your own country, and in Indonesia during the tsunami, serves as a reminder to me to consider seriously the filing of an application to be of service to *Médecins Sans Frontières*, an organization that at this time benefits only from my modest financial support. And you are also a man of Jewish descent, am I correct?"

"Yes. But why—?"

"My parents were friendly with a Jewish man—Austrian, not Israeli—when I was a young boy in Beirut. He was a merchant involved in silk and linens, and we ate in his home upon occasion. I am Christian—not Muslim or Druse—and thus did not have restrictions against eating pork, but neither did this man and his family. His name was Emanuel Mandelbaum, and he loved electrical appliances and had acquired many—vegetable choppers, small ovens, *grillades*, egg boilers. In his basement, he repaired appliances for friends and neighbors. He was a fastidious man, and, remembering now the deftness of his fingers—they were quite small, and what I think you call 'stubbed'—it occurs to me that he would have made an excellent surgeon."

"Was he a survivor?"

"A survivor?"

"Of the camps."

"Of course."

Doctor Chehade reached into an inside jacket pocket and, like a magician, so deft were his moves, he withdrew a piece of equipment which he quickly attached to his forehead. It was a head lamp, Ira saw, and it gave off a long rod-like beam of pure white light. Doctor Chehade directed the beam of light onto the palm of his left hand so that he could adjust its intensity. Then he removed the bandage from Ira's damaged eye, after which, very gently, he probed the area surrounding the eye with his fingers.

"Very good," he said. "Excellent."

He turned out the room's overhead light, closed the door. In his left hand he held a small piece of glass, which he moved back and forth in the space between Ira's eye and the light that came from the head lamp.

"No more split-lens ophthalmoscopes?" Ira asked.

"We have not used those for many years," Doctor Chehade replied. "This is a convex lens, you see, and creates a *virtual* image, but an image that is indefinitely more accurate."

"You mean infinitely—*infinitely* more accurate."

"Of course."

The lens, which Doctor Chehade rotated between thumb and

forefinger, looked to Ira like a large cat's eye. Ira closed his good eye, and when he did, saw nothing but gray, as if a sheet of slate had been slipped into a slot behind his retina in the way a photographer slipped a photographic plate into a camera.

Doctor Chehade was replacing the bandage, washing his hands. "It is as I thought," he said. "The healing has already begun, but we will not know for some time yet how much regeneration we will have. You may dispense with the bandage tomorrow, nor will you require an eye patch afterward. I have ordered antibiotic drops, to prevent infection and inflammation, and I am confident that you will regain, at the least, some portion of your peripheral vision."

"And after that—?"

Doctor Chehade shrugged. "Who knows? Time, Doctor Farb. Time must become our friend. In four to six weeks, we will know more. But I would look forward, frankly, to a healing period of at least several months."

"Great," Ira said. "And I had a heart attack too, right?"

"A minor infarction we discovered while preparing you for surgery, one which is, as we say truly, of little or no consequence. Doctor Guérard estimates that it probably occurred some time within the past twelve months. Perhaps you recall some unusual indigestion, or some fleeting pain you attributed to exercise, or—"

"S.B.D.," Ira said.

"S.B.D.?"

"Silent But Deadly—what we called silent flatulence when I was a boy."

"That is very good—I will remember it," Doctor Chehade said. "S.B.D. But Doctor Guérard is not concerned for your heart, for it is a kind of miracle—what we call the wisdom of the body, yes?—how one can function and live on with only minor portions of the heart muscle remaining alive. Doctor Guérard will urge you to change your habits, but if you do or if you do not, we expect you will reach a ripe maturity. Were there a danger more imminent, he would not release you back to the world."

"Great news," Ira said.

"Often, too, the fibrosis of the retina can cause a tension— a *tractional* detachment—that may cause the retina to detach again," Doctor Chehade said. "Still, I am optimistic."

"Why?"

"*Why?*" Doctor Chehade laughed. "Because I am an excellent surgeon and an optimistic human being—that is why!" he declared. "And because I like you. Because I sense, given how we were drawn to each other, that this is a feeling quite mutual. But let me ask you something else—my true reason for remaining until you regained more thoroughly your consciousness. The question I have been preparing to offer is this: What are your allegiances to the State of Israel?"

"Excuse me?" Ira said. "What does the State of Israel have to do with my surgery?"

"I feel a responsibility, as a man of Middle Eastern origin—a man from a civilized Arab nation—to talk to my Jewish friends about this when occasion presents itself. I talk with you as I have often talked with colleagues in the hospital who are of Jewish extraction. I trust you will believe that I am not singling you out."

"I'm an American," Ira said.

"Of course you are."

"And a Jew. Yes, I'm a Jew."

"Well, I knew that, but I am glad you have decided to clarify your status. Honesty is a requirement of any true friendship."

"What I meant to say is that I'm a Jew, but not an observant or practicing Jew," Ira said, and immediately wondered why he was offering this information. "Being Jewish does not inform my ordinary, waking life in any particular way," he went on. "I don't go to synagogue or observe the holidays—not even those most Jews observe—what we call the High Holy Days, the New Year and our Day of Atonement."

"I understand," Doctor Chehade said. "Of course. I have met Jewish people such as yourself—Americans as well as French and English—and their habits of living conform to your description. You should be assured that I remain a great admirer of your people. Sometimes I think that I admire you more than many Jewish people themselves do—those who, *malheureusement*, seem to have forgotten who they are, and where they come from, and why they are here."

Doctor Chehade steepled his hands below his lips. "You are, you see, a people who believe in One God, who is, of course, the God of all creation. You are a people with great respect for learning, and with traditions of charity, justice, and hospitality very much like those of my own people. You have stayed together—a true community, with common bonds, beliefs, and rituals—despite oppression and plagues, and without, until this past century, a land of your own. The most excellent doctors I have known, both here and in my own homeland, have been Jewish. I am proud to call myself your friend and that you have chosen to listen to me, yet at the same time I recognize that you have become fatigued from your ordeals and also, perhaps, confused as to the direction of my discourse. Therefore, I will arrive swiftly at my conclusion."

Doctor Chehade stepped back and when he spoke, his voice became stronger, as if he were speaking not only to Ira but to other men, perhaps ten or twelve of whom had entered the room and were gathered around Ira's bed. Ira wanted to explain why it was that a secular Jew—a *lapsed* Jew?—was not considered a sinner. But he wondered too: had he somehow—by his behavior, his words, his eagerness to be friends—invited the moment he was now living in?

"I feel it incumbent upon me when I am with Jewish friends—" Doctor Chehade said "—and I want you to listen very carefully to what I say now—to inform you that although the State of Israel will, in the future as in the past, win many battles, it will not win the war. It cannot."

Doctor Chehade took Ira's free hand in both his own.

"I see that you are eager to sleep again," he said, "and I trust it is not because I am boring you. *Par conséquent*, let me end our dialogue by asserting that I understand that this has been a difficult time for you, and in such a time I do not intend to add to your burdens. Still, while you must understand that *I* certainly am not against you or your people, you must also understand that history is."

Doctor Chehade left the room. Ira closed his good eye. He dreamt of leaving the hospital, of walking the streets of Brooklyn, or Nice—or Jerusalem!—with his wife, and of describing for her what had happened. *But damn—why didn't I see it coming?* he heard himself say, and when he did, his wife told him that at least he had the words right, and when he imagined her saying this, he began to laugh out loud—to laugh so hard that a nurse entered his room and asked if he was all right.

"Oh yes," he said. He touched his eye patch and began laughing again. "But I was wondering if you could tell me—please?— why it is that I didn't *see* it coming."

The Turetzky Trio

Bart parked his car in a garage under a Monoprix store near the center of town, then made his way down toward the market place. He descended slowly, glancing into windows of shops—olive oil and olive wood products, eyeglasses, hardware, perfumes, lingerie, auto supplies—and into open doorways that revealed courtyards, fountains, laundry hanging between buildings. He loved the curving stairways, the chipped stucco walls, the hard unevenness of the stone under his feet, the sound of the French language in his ears.

It was the first time he had been in Grasse since he and his wife Marjorie had brought their two children here nearly two dozen years before for a tour of one of the city's perfumeries, and when he arrived at the lower part of town—La Place Aux Aires—he was pleased to find that the market place was essentially as he remembered it: long rows of vendors, their fruits, vegetables, fish, meats, cheeses, linens, soaps, and spices on display, the vendors shouting the praises of their products: *poisson frais…! légumes directement du jardin…! bon prix…! bon marché…!*

Marjorie, a senior editor specializing in cookbooks at a New York publishing house, had been reading in the garden of their vacation home when he left. When he kissed her goodby, on the top of her head, she had turned to him and—out of anger?

desire?—had pulled him down and pressed her mouth against his, hard.

The warmth of the sun, on his back and shoulders now that he had passed into the open air of the plaza, reminded him of the force of Marjorie's hand on the back of his neck, and of how at dusk the evening before the two of them had, on their balcony, held hands while they watched lights come on across the valley below and in Cannes. It was as if they were trying, against probability, to recreate feelings like those they had known in a time before they had married, before they had had children, before the AIDS pandemic had erupted, before they had begun indulging in their liaisons.

He had a sudden desire to return to the car, to drive back to Marjorie, and to talk with her about doubts and fears that had been with him lately—about the many things he felt he had not, as a man and a doctor, done or achieved. But why such a distinctly unfamiliar urge? Was it his age—he would be sixty in three months—and what he had not told Marjorie, or, more important, talked with a cardiologist about—the occasional shortness of breath he had been experiencing recently? If he lost ten pounds, though—if he exercised more regularly and ate more sensibly, he had confidence that all would be well. Still, he wondered: if he left the world now, would Marjorie miss him?

More likely, he thought, she would be relieved. Doubtless she would grieve for a while and would talk with the children about what a good and admirable man he was. Surely she would emphasize what the children already knew: that he was highly esteemed by others, especially by those in the world of AIDS with whom he worked. Truth be told, though, he was a good and admirable man mostly—*only?*—when he was doing for those who were *not* family to him. When he was with a patient, or mentoring a medical student—*that* was when he felt good about himself, when he came truly alive.

He went on his round of the stalls, made his purchases—

bread, fish, vegetables, cheese, wine—and when, his *panier* heavy with goods, he was ready to start the climb back toward the center of town, he found that he was feeling faint. In the shade of the market's arcade, he took a seat at a café and asked for a *pastis,* after which he ordered *la formule*: melon with cured ham, followed by a *pavé* of grilled rumpsteak with *pommes frites.*

He ate slowly, and when he was done, ordered coffee. The coffee was rich and black, and drinking it, he found himself craving a cigarette. He asked his waiter if there was a *tabac* nearby, patted his pockets to indicate he had no more—"*Je n'en ai plus*"—and the waiter returned a minute later with a pack of *Gitanes*—*Fumer Tue* in bold letters on the pack's front—tapped out a single cigarette and lit it for Bart.

Bart drew in on the cigarette, imagined his thoughts, like fumes, floating upward and dissolving in the balm of day. He put on his aviator-style sunglasses and looked around. Who *was* this man, he imagined people asking. An expatriate writer living in a villa on the *Côte d'Azur*? A CIA operative posing as a retired businessman? A gay man sentenced to death, T-cells nearing zero, spending his last days in the place he loved most in the world? An aging actor who had, perhaps, been friends with Jean Renoir and Jean Cocteau, and with Cocteau's lover, the actor Jean Marais…?

Marais had been living in Spéracèdes when Bart and Marjorie had lived there for several months nearly four decades before, though they had never seen him. They had never seen Picasso either, though he lived a few miles away, in Mougins, and though they had several times parked nearby and walked around the walls of his estate, hoping to catch a glimpse of him. When, four months after arriving in Spéracèdes, they decided to get married, they had sent Picasso a check for fifty dollars, telling him this was a wedding gift to themselves and asking if there were anything they could purchase for the fifty dollars. What they received back, now framed and hanging on a wall of their bedroom, was the cancelled check itself, endorsed on the back, a small dove-with-olive-branch sketched beneath Picasso's signature.

It occurred to Bart that Marais could, despite his fame, have lived on in Spéracèdes forever without having anyone from the village, much less a tourist, ever see him or bother him (a young man they regularly saw in town performed Marais's errands), just as Bart could sit at this outdoor café forever without having anyone talk to him, or bother him.

He asked the waiter for another cigarette, thought of stories he had heard of husbands and wives who said they were going to the corner to get a pack of cigarettes, and who never returned and were never found. He could notify his hospital—Montefiore, in the Bronx—that he had decided to take early retirement—that they should send him whatever papers needed signing and should deposit his pension checks in his bank account.

He drank the last of his coffee—the bitter grounds tasted wonderful, would mask the cigarette taste—and, signalling to the waiter for the check, realized that a woman, a cup of coffee at her lips, was watching him. She smiled, inclined her head slightly.

He paid the check, walked to the woman's table. "You're Leah Turetzky, aren't you?" he said.

"Yes."

"May I join you?"

She gestured with a hand, indicating that he could.

"My wife and I saw you at Lincoln Center three or four years ago," he said. "You played the Schubert B flat Trio, one of my wife's favorites, and I remember that you wore a burgundy gown, trimmed with black lace. We were planning to go to your concert tomorrow evening, but a question first, if you'll allow me: Why The Turetzky Duo instead of Trio? When we were in Cannes the day before yesterday, my wife and I saw a poster and…"

He was aware that he was talking quickly, and that he was

not, as he usually was in these situations, relaxed and confident. He waited a few seconds, but she waited too, her gaze steady, slightly bemused.

"Actually, my wife and I arrived only a week ago," he said, "but when I saw the poster, I wondered about what happened."

"My husband Alex died five weeks ago."

Bart blinked. "I'm sorry. I didn't mean to be so glib, and—" He stopped. "I don't really know what to say."

"He died in Paris, which was his favorite city," Leah said. "We'd been to the opera—*Manon*—and we were drinking champagne, a custom of ours after attending opera—and he suddenly sat up in bed, opened his mouth wide, said a very quiet 'Oh!' and then was gone. It was his heart, of course—his first attack, and his last. The pain seemed minimal, though how is anyone to know really?"

She took out a cigarette, handed Bart a matchbook so he could light it for her. "We decided to go ahead with the tour, Eugene and I—Eugene is Alex's brother, our violinist—and all things considered, this seemed best."

"I see that I've been indiscreet," he said. "I should leave."

"Why?"

The crisp directness of her question set him at ease. "I'm Bart Schneider," he said, and he reached across the table to shake her hand. "I'm a physician. My wife and I are here for a few months, on a mini-sabbatical. I work with AIDS patients."

"You have a wife?"

"Why yes—I thought I mentioned her."

"But only four times." She laughed, and when she did, Bart found himself laughing with her.

"You look younger when you laugh," Leah said. "Before his death, Alex had not laughed for eight months."

"You kept count?!"

"Of course not," she said. "My goodness, but you're literal. *Je rigolais avec toi.*"

"I don't understand."

142

"I was playing—making a joke with you," she said. "You speak French, don't you? I would have thought, watching you with the waiter, that you did."

"I did—I do," he said. "Look—can we start over? Your husband died five weeks ago. What then? I mean, did you return to the States? Was there a funeral—a service of some kind?"

"I sent Alex home—his body, that is—but kept his cello. It's a Goffriller, and quite valuable. It's probably worth more than the two of us—the *three* of us, for that matter—alive or dead. Shall I tell you about it?"

"If you want."

He sat back and, while she talked, he watched her mouth. Her lips—thin, wide, sharply articulated and slightly bow-shaped—reminded him of Garbo's, and he made a mental note to say this to her later on. It was the supreme and ever effective compliment—to compare a woman's features to that of a movie star, especially to one from a bygone era: Lombard, Astor, Del Rio, Harlow, Bacall, Hayworth, Gardner, Brooks...

"Alex's instrument was built in Venice, in the early eighteenth century," she said. "The body, neck, ribs, and scroll are of maple, the top is of spruce, and the end piece, tail piece, and pegs are of rosewood. Am I boring you?"

"Not possible."

"The soul of the cello, however—" she said "—the technical term is just that—*l'âme*—a slender piece of wood that determines tone and timbre, perhaps a quarter of an inch thick, and set into the body between the back and the belly just below the foot of the bridge, is of pine." She drew in on her cigarette. "Alex often said that a fine cello is like a good woman: warm and capricious. Nor does it like to be forced. The less power you apply, the more you get."

"I was remembering the photo on the poster—for your concert," he said. "It seems to have been taken some years ago, yet I was thinking of how much more attractive you are now."

"So what I've been wondering about is this," she said. "Do I, at the start of my career as widow, remind you of women in previous generations, afflicted with TB—the Camilles of their time, who, flush-cheeked and dying, represented an ideal of beauty? Will AIDS now do for some of us what TB used to do?"

Bart felt himself stiffen. "Hardly," he said. "AIDS ravages all those it visits in godawful ways, though if you were in the early stages, there would be no visible difference. AIDS has a long incubation time, thank the Lord."

"Have I offended?" she asked. "I am often more direct than is necessary."

"One of my most extraordinary patients was a musical savant," Bart offered.

"*Was?*"

"He passed away several years ago, when he was twenty-four. His name was Ethan Goldfarb."

"His instrument?"

"Yours—the piano—which is why he came to mind. Most musical savants are, of course, autistic."

"When we traveled by plane or train," Leah said, "we'd buy a seat for Alex's cello, and, on wide-body planes, for example— across oceans—it would sit between us."

"As if it were your child?" Bart asked.

"More as if we were a *ménage à trois*," she said. "But tell me about these musical savants."

"Though many of them can hardly speak or sign their names in any but the crudest way, they can, after listening to a sonata a few times, reproduce it faithfully, and with what seems genuine musical feeling. Most show this talent before the age of one, most are male, most are visually impaired, and they *all* play piano."

"You've studied them obviously."

"I knew Ethan."

"Do you know all your patients in the way you knew him?"

"I hope so, though often AIDS patients will wander from clinic to clinic and doctor to doctor, with stops in between that further debilitate them. And there's also this, that doctors have favorites too. Ethan was a favorite."

"If you'll permit me a somewhat cold calculus—like Ethan, the other patients who come to you with AIDS—they all die, don't they?"

"No. Things have been changing in recent years. Antiretrovirals have made an enormous difference. Ethan, sad to say, was one of the last patients I lost."

"Yet it seems wonderful to me to have known so many people in their time of dying," she said. "I'm envious."

"Don't be," he said. "I don't miss attending funerals, and I attended hundreds of them. No pleasure, believe me, although I admit that I do sometimes find myself missing the years when the epidemic itself was exploding—when there was a sense of camaraderie among the doctors and nurses I worked with that was exhilarating, when we were discovering things nobody knew anything about, when we were desperate to save the world." Bart stubbed out his cigarette. "But it was a terrible, godawful world."

"So it would seem."

"But you and I—this conversation—we're going down a road that's much too dark for such a pretty day, don't you think?"

"It occurs to me that where Alex is now, he and Ethan may have found one another, and that the boy may have replaced me as Alex's accompanist."

"How long will you be staying in Grasse?"

"We don't stay here. We *play* here. We're staying a few miles away, in Tourettes-sur-Loup. Do you know it?"

"My favorite in the area, actually, whereas Grasse, which has its merits, is—"

"Is what?"

"Camus called it the capital of barbers' assistants," Bart said.

"We're here until Sunday. There's our concert tomorrow night, and on Sunday morning we leave for Genoa."

"And between now and tomorrow night—?" Bart waited,

and when she did not respond, spoke again: "You and Alex's brother must be practicing together more frequently now that you have a new repertoire—"

"I should revise what I said before, about your young man being Alex's accompanist. In the beginning, you see—in the time of Corelli, Mozart, Haydn—it was the violin and cello that were considered to be accompanying the piano."

"Have you thought of going on tour as a soloist?"

"To be alone on a stage, or on tour, has always seemed to me a kind of death. At the same time, I do dread the possibility that I may now be linked to Eugene forever, without Alex between us."

"Eugene is difficult?"

"Eugene is in love with me."

"And—?"

"And I'm not in love with him, though on the day of Alex's death I was a bit out of my mind, so that when we were alone after the ambulance had taken Alex away, and Eugene comforted me…" She stopped. "But why am I telling you this? Can you explain that for me, doctor?"

"Trust," Bart said. "Or an intimation of trust."

"I doubt it. That's a very romantic notion—a very *male* romantic notion, I've come to believe."

"You've clearly been through an ordeal, and—"

"Eugene and I have a practice scheduled for later today." She glanced at her watch. "We prefer early mornings or late afternoons, so what I was wondering is this: We can continue our conversation here, or—if you have the time and interest—I could make you a cup of coffee. The apartment I'm staying in has a splendid view—and that way you would also get to see Alex's cello."

When he woke, Leah was sitting a few feet from the bed, reading, and he saw, with relief—the shutters were open—that it was still daylight. Leah wore a thin, peach-colored robe. The cello, resting upright in its stand, was beside her.

"I can't make a decision," he said, "as to which is more beautiful—you or the cello."

"Well, given its age, the cello certainly has shown itself to have greater staying power," she said. She set her book down. "But we need to do something for you before you return home. Stay here, please."

She returned a minute later carrying a basin and pitcher. She poured water into the basin, dipped a washcloth into the basin, squeezed out excess water, and, starting with his toes, began washing him. The washcloth was warm.

"There's nothing quite like it, is there, when it's good the first time," she said.

She dipped the cloth in the basin again, began washing his thighs and groin. Bart moved his hand so that it rested between her legs. She lifted his hand, set it back on the bed.

"Your hands are very strong," he said.

"We have Messrs. Czerny and Hanon to thank for that," she said. "I enjoy caring for you, you see—allowing myself to be tender. When I have this—you and me, in this way—I feel I can go on. Much of the time, of course, the prospect of joining Alex seems quite natural and inviting."

"I don't understand."

She stood. "I'll make coffee," she said. "You need to be alert on the drive home."

When she returned with coffee, he sat up. "The French are a very practical people," she said. "It's not the night of love that matters most, they say, but the cup of coffee in the morning."

"But it's not morning."

"You would notice that, wouldn't you," she said. "But while you were sleeping, I found myself thinking about divorce. In the States these days, five minutes after a married man or woman falls in love with someone else, they divorce, and the family is destroyed, the children affected for the rest of their lives. Here, though things are changing—Americanizing, if you will—a man can still have his *petite amie à coté,* a woman can have her liaisons—her *cinq à sept*—and families stay together. Much more practical—much more *sane*—don't you think?"

"I've been married to the same woman for nearly forty years."

"Which reminds me," Leah said. "Tomorrow night, after the concert, please don't come backstage to congratulate me."

"Because—?"

"Because if you do, your wife, who I assume is a not unperceptive woman, will know at once."

"And tomorrow, before the concert? I could—"

"I am occupied all day tomorrow."

"Then this afternoon was—?"

"Yes."

He set his cup down on the night table, pulled her down to him.

"You have an admirable quotient of violence in you," she said a short while later. "I like that."

"I noticed."

Bart tried to pull her to him again, but she stepped away from the bed.

"I think we should leave things as they were," she said. "You should go now. The afternoon has been wonderful. You are a dear and fascinating man. I will think of you often."

"Do you say that to all the boys?" he asked.

"Don't be vulgar," she said. "Please. What we had *was* wonderful. Now it's over, and we must be practical. I will think of you often, and with great kindness."

Lakewood, New Jersey

Through the many months of what their hospitals called 'assisted reproductive services,' my daughters Carolyn and Michelle kept me informed about 'options': in vitro fertilization, embryo cyropreservation, intracytoplasmic sperm injection, intrauterine insemination, donor oocytes, donor sperm, electroejaculation, and a long menu of other high-tech procedures.

What I insisted on—my only condition for the zero-interest, zero-repayment loans I offered—was that if child number one came into the world whole and healthy, they would each promise to try to have at least one additional child.

"What you want to do," I said, "is to keep a spare on hand," to which suggestion they asked if I was joking, and did I really take such a pessimistic ('tragic' was Carolyn's word) view of their futures. Or: was I recommending they have more than one child because of my experience in having been an only child?

That probably had something to do with it, I admitted—how not?—but this was about them, not me, and I was just trying to be practical.

All went well. Carolyn (at Mount Sinai Hospital, in New York City) had a boy, Michelle (at Beth Israel, in Boston) had a girl (the babies born four months apart), and two years after their first children were born, they became pregnant again (within a month of each other), and the second time around, and without benefit of assisted reproductive services, things reversed: Michelle had a boy, and Carolyn had a girl.

My first two grandchildren, Amos and Shira, were born eight years ago, two years after their grandmother, Helene, my wife of thirty-two years, passed away. The next two, Deborah and Saul, were born five years ago, and the happy endings to these chapters in our lives—four healthy grandchildren, two fit and healthy mothers—enabled me to return certain memories to where they'd been living for most of my adult life: in a seldom visited, windowless room of my mind.

Then, starting seven months ago, when the last remaining relative of my parents' generation, my Uncle Herschel, died (he was ninety-three, and was hit by a car at the intersection of Broadway and 89th Street in Manhattan, when, crossing the street, he bent down to pick up a dime), the door to that windowless room opened wide, and feelings I thought I'd put away forever, especially after Herschel's son Joey died more than forty years ago, tumbled out, and with a power that, like one of Herschel's famous punches—he'd been a terrific amateur boxer, a Golden Gloves and AAU champion—stunned.

When I was growing up in Brooklyn during the years following World War Two (I was born in 1938), my mother, Herschel's youngest sister, worked as a registered nurse at Kings County Hospital. My father worked at odd jobs, mostly as a floor salesman at shoe stores on Flatbush Avenue, and sometimes, with Herschel, as a runner for the guys who controlled the gambling and numbers rackets in our section of Brooklyn.

When I was five months old, my father contracted mumps. My mother claimed he caught it from hanging out with low-life; my father claimed she passed it on to him after exchanging saliva samples with one of the doctors she worked with. Though I stopped listening to their arguments about *why* I was an only child early on, my mother could still get to me when she told me what, in memory, she seemed to do every day of my life: that she loved me so much that if anything ever happened to me, she didn't know *what* she'd do to herself.

"If you go, Marty, then I follow," she'd say. "You can count on it."

I'd say stuff back to her—that there was nothing to worry about, that I was in great shape, that I wished she'd stop talking this way—but nothing helped. When I was fourteen years old, though, I finally said something I'd been fantasizing saying for a long time, and I can date the event from the fact that it was the year my elementary school, Public School Number 246 changed into *Junior* High School Number 246. Because my friends and I were eighth graders who'd gone to P.S. 246 since kindergarten, we were allowed to go straight to high school instead of having to spend ninth grade in junior high the way new kids entering the school that year would have to.

Three weeks after my fourteenth birthday, on graduation night, when my mother found out that my friends and I were planning to go across the river to New Jersey—to Minsky's for a burlesque show—she threw a fit. Over her dead body would she let me go, she said, because she knew the kinds of jokers who hung around places like that and preyed on pretty boys like me, after which she added her usual line about not knowing what she'd do to herself if anything happened to me.

Because I felt humiliated by the *thought* of having to tell my friends my mother wouldn't let me go to a burlesque show with them, I said that if something happened to me, she could always *buy* a new child to replace me.

"Now what the hell is that supposed to mean?" she said.

"You know," I said.

"I know what?" she said.

"If anything happens to me, you could *buy* a new son the way Uncle Herschel and Aunt Rose bought Joey," I said, "and the way all the others do—the ones you and Doctor Margolies sell—one of your black market babies."

She was so astonished, she just stood where she was, her mouth open in amazement, and sensing I'd wounded her the way I'd often hoped to, I added that because we were family, she could probably get a discount.

That did it. She came at me, slammed me against our break-front—I heard stuff shatter—raked her fingernails down my face, and then, before I could cover up, she started in slapping at me with both hands, one after the other—left right, left right—while screaming that I had a mind as dirty as my mouth, and if I ever dared talk this way to her again I'd wind up at the bottom of the Gowanus Canal in cement boots, after which she'd put on her best dress and her silk stockings and go out dancing. My father stayed in his easy chair like the lump he usually was, a low moaning sound coming from somewhere inside his chest.

"And let me tell you something else, you ungrateful little stinker," my mother said when she'd stopped slapping me around. "Nobody knows the risks we take. Nobody knows, do you hear me? We bring happiness into people's lives that they shower blessings on us for, and nobody knows, do you understand? Nobody ever knows."

"I know," I said.

"And the *good* we do for people—helping young girls out of the worst kind of trouble, and young wives wanting to be mothers and cursed by some fucking heartless god to be sterile their whole lives—most of them from the best families, for your information, and I mean the *very* best—the daughters of judges and doctors and even rabbis—and nobody ever knows all the good we do."

"And all the money we make!" my father chimed in, which made my mother look at him as if he were some drunken fool who'd wandered in from the street.

"You go wash up, and don't forget to use hydrogen perox-ide," she said. Then, to my father: "And you—who invited *you* to this party? Because you can drop dead for all I care. In fact, the both of you can, and I mean it this time, to have this little *pisher* talk to me the way he did…"

152

Which words seemed to give my father the excuse he was waiting for to take a turn whacking me around while proclaiming that *nobody* talked to his wife the way I did without having to deal with him. But I got away easily—I was always too quick for him—and locked myself in the bathroom, where I cleaned out the scratches on my face.

By the time I came out my mother was gone, who knew where, so I headed out to meet my friends, and we went to Minsky's and had a great old time. When I explained the marks on my face by saying I'd picked up this wild chick in Greenwich Village—a real tiger—and had started celebrating early by taming the beast in her, my friends were skeptical, but not totally disbelieving—I had a reputation for taking dares and doing wild things back then—and I doubt that it would have occurred to any of them to think it was my mother who'd done the damage.

My mother and I never mentioned Doctor Margolies or black market babies again, but I think it broke her heart—not that I knew about what she did, because how could I not have known, given all the talk that went on over our phone about babies and money and lawyers and when and where deliveries and exchanges would take place, but because by saying what I'd said I'd broken some unwritten agreement we'd had about never acknowledging out loud that she did what she did.

But there was something else at work too, because if we'd talked about it, I would have agreed that though she and Doctor Margolies may have been breaking laws, they weren't *hurting* anyone: that they were, in fact, doing what my mother said they were doing—helping some people out of jams while helping other people fulfill their dreams. Plus—the main thing, from my point of view—they were giving a child who would have been stigmatized as a bastard, a life that child would never otherwise have had. I'd heard my mother whispering her justifications and rationalizations into the phone to one or another of her sisters (she had three sisters and one other brother besides

Herschel), or to Doctor Margolies, a thousand times, and except for when she'd cover the mouthpiece with her hand and go more hush-hush if I passed through the foyer, where our phone was, I never thought much about the effect on me of what she did, partly because I'd heard her talk about other doctors and nurses who were doing the same thing, so that it just seemed what people did to avoid being at the mercy of adoption agencies and the crap and lousy choices they put you through.

What I began to see, though—what became clear around the time of Herschel's death—was that one reason I got so angry with my mother wasn't because of what she and Doctor Margolies *did*—in a weird way, I was proud of her for being a kind of outlaw who risked her life and career to rescue people from misery—but because I'd always wanted to *be* one of the children she'd bought and sold.

Because if a mother and father paid large amounts of money and risked going to jail to make you their child, they must really have wanted you and loved you.

"Dogs fuck dogs and make more dogs," I'd hear my mother say to people she was providing babies for. "It's *raising* the child that makes you a parent, and you'll see—the minute you hold that precious package in your arms, you'll fall in love with it and feel it's yours and will be yours forever."

My cousin Joey had been a black market baby—born, bought, and sold into our family before I was born—and because he was my favorite cousin, it made me wish I could have come into the world the way he did: illicitly, and in a way that, once he discovered his true origins, he could, as I saw it, have had it both ways—he could be grateful to his parents, my Uncle Herschel and Aunt Rose, for wanting him so much that they made him their child even though he wasn't biologically theirs, and he could also have held a trump card against them if he ever needed one by being able to say: You're not my *real* parents.

But I didn't love Joey mainly because he'd been a black market baby. He'd become my hero years before I knew this about him, when he was fighting in the Pacific as a navigator in a B-24 over Saipan and New Guinea. When I wrote letters to him, he answered them, and at the end of each letter always said that my prayers were keeping him and his buddies alive—that they were fighting to keep us *all* alive and free—and that I should keep my chin up and the home fires burning.

When he came home from the war in 1945, he brought me a box of souvenirs—insignias, medals, a compass in a flip-open metal case, a small gnarled item wrapped in plastic that he said was the ear of a Japanese soldier (while I was sleeping one night, my mother took it from my room and threw it away), three bullets still filled with gunpowder, and his dog tags, which I wore on a chain around my neck.

And he told me again—this was at a welcome home party his parents made, a big red-white-and-blue sign over the entrance to their apartment building—WELCOME HOME OUR HERO JOEY!—that it was thinking about me that had kept him going when he never knew if, in the next minute or hour, he was going to live or die. He just kept telling himself, "If I stay alive, I bet there'll be another letter from Marty waiting for me at the base when I get back, and you know what? I lived for your letters, Marty! I showed them to my buddies and they agreed that you've got one hell of a talent there and are gonna be a great writer some day."

"*Really?*" I'd say.

"You bet," he'd say, and chuck me on the shoulder. "When it comes to words, you got the gift. But there was this, too, see—because most of the other guys got their letters from their wives or sweethearts, what they worried about—almost more than getting shot down and captured, which we figured would be worse than dying, the way the Japs did things—was if their women would stay true to them, them being away from home for so long."

"Did you see any of them die?" I asked.

"I saw some of my buddies die," he said, and as soon as he did, he walked away to the table where the booze was, poured himself a drink, and began slapping people on the back and telling them how great it was to be home.

Joey went to college on the G.I. Bill—to Brooklyn College, where he was a star on the basketball team (he'd been high scorer for his high school team when he'd played at Erasmus before the war), and I'd go to all his home games. He always left me comp tickets at the door, and I usually sat with Herschel, who'd go wild whenever Joey scored, but even wilder when a referee called a foul on Joey that Hershel disagreed with. He'd scream and curse at the ref, and ask him who his optometrist was, or if the other coach or some bookie was paying him off, and if a ref looked his way, Herschel would stand up and point right at him and tell the guy to meet him outside after the game and he'd show him what playing fair was all about.

I think Joey looked up to his father as much as I looked up to Joey, though when I once said something to my mother about how much Joey admired Herschel, and about what a great man he was, she sneered.

"My brother has his fans, that's for sure, but don't count me as one of them," she said. "I love him, I suppose, and he probably loves me in his cockeyed way, but mostly Herschel's an operator who's always been hot after the buck."

"But he was a great boxer," I protested, and talked about all the trophies in his apartment, and the signed photos on the walls of him with famous fighters—Jack Dempsey, Max Baer, Benny Leonard, Gene Fullmer, Carmen Basilio, Jimmy Braddock, and lots of others.

"He got around, Herschel did," my mother acknowledged. "And he had some talent and lots of grit, I'll give that to him."

"Joey says he knew *all* the great fighters, even Joe Louis!"

"He knows Louis," my mother said, and looked at me in a

funny way that made me think she knew I was thinking about Louis's training camp in Lakewood, New Jersey, where I'd been with Herschel and Joey, and which was near the place where a lot of the young women who got pregnant, and who my mother and Doctor Margolies worked with, stayed before they gave birth.

After Joey graduated from college, he got a start in the garment business through a guy who owed Herschel a favor from gambling debts Herschel had helped him with, but a guy who also said that with Joey's record—a war hero, and a star athlete—along with his terrific personality and good looks (he was a dead ringer, the man said, for the actor John Garfield, who'd grown up in the man's neighborhood when his name was Jacob Garfinkle)—he'd be a natural.

Which he was, and within less than two years he'd moved up from salesman, to head of sales, to full partner. By this time, he'd also married—Carol Schifrin, a very pretty lady who'd gone to Adelphi College and ran a travel agency with her parents— and they'd had a house built for them in Scarsdale they helped design. Although my mother and father didn't like to praise much connected with Herschel or Joey, they couldn't keep from being in awe at what they called the dream-come-true house and life Joey and Carol had. And on rare occasions my mother would accord Joey the highest compliment you could pay a guy in those days. "He's good to his parents—I have to give him that," she'd say. "He's good to Rose and Herschel, and that goes a long way with me."

We visited Joey for his Open House party in Scarsdale, and, since everyone I knew until then lived in small one or two bedroom apartments (I didn't have a single friend or relative who owned a private home), the house seemed incredible. It had four separate bathrooms (including one attached to the guest room), sky-lights in all the upstairs bedrooms, a landscaped backyard with an in-ground swimming pool, and—my favorite part—a finished basement with a bar, a first-class stereo system, an enormous TV, and a workout room where, along with weights and barbells, there was a gym-quality heavy bag, a speed bag that hung down from the ceiling, and, the bag Herschel loved most of all, a free-standing *reflex* speed bag.

After school sometimes, I'd take the subway into Manhattan, to Eighth Avenue and West 38th Street, to visit Joey, and no matter when I did, he'd stop work and tell his secretaries to hold his phone calls so he could show me around. The main factory floor was over a hundred feet long and about thirty to forty feet wide, with two long tables running its length on which there were bolts of cloth spread out flat and stacked high that the cutters worked on. Around three sides of the room were dozens of sewing machines where women—mostly Spanish, but with a few elderly Jewish ladies too—assembled and stitched together material that came from the cutting tables.

Joey's company manufactured sports shirts mostly, the kinds with little emblems on their breast pockets of animals—crocodiles (this was before Lacoste trademarked them), ducks, sharks, tigers, bears, lions—or sports stuff: baseballs, footballs, basketballs, tennis balls, tennis rackets, golf balls, golf clubs—and Joey would give me a tour of the place, introduce me to workers, tell me what they did, and praise them for how good they were at their jobs. He'd always ask which of his new line of shirts I liked best, and before I left he'd give me a box with three or four shirts packed up in white tissue paper.

When I was fifteen, and playing JV basketball at Erasmus, Joey came to some of my games, gave me pointers, mostly about passing and defense, which he called the dying arts of the game, and when the season was over, and I'd made it up to varsity for the last half-dozen games and the playoffs (we went to the quarterfinals of the city championship that year, and had two guys on our team, Doug Moe and Julie Cohen, who eventually wound up being All-American college players), to celebrate my season, he and his father got permission from my mother to take me out to Lakewood for a weekend, where Joe Louis, well past his prime and in big trouble with ex-wives and back taxes (and drugs, we'd later learn), was training in the hopes of making another comeback, even though, while still champ, he'd already been badly shown up by Billy Conn and Jersey Joe Walcott, and, in his initial comeback attempts, had been badly beaten by Ezzard Charles and Rocky Marciano.

I'd been to the training camp twice before, but when I was much younger, and this time being there was a dream come true. I was able to go jogging with Joey, Herschel, and the fighters and trainers every morning—Louis too—and to spend my day in the gym, working out on the machines and watching the fighters spar. I ate my meals at the training tables with them, and it felt wonderful to see the way people still looked up to Herschel, and lapped up the stories he told about the way things had been in the fight game in what he called the golden olden days.

That year Joey had gotten Jackie Robinson to endorse a line of shirts—long-sleeve shirts with leopard skin patterns—and he'd brought a few boxes of the shirts with him, before they were put on sale in stores, and gave them out to everyone, including Louis, and they were a big hit. At night, after the fighters went to sleep, Herschel and the managers and trainers would reminisce and argue and drink until the early hours of the morning, when—their way of signalling it was time to hit the hay— one of them would tell the old story of Max Baer stumbling back to his corner when Dempsey was acting as one of his seconds, and telling Dempsey, "I see three of them." "Hit the one in the middle," Dempsey advised.

Although Herschel had never fought professionally, he'd been a top-flight amateur boxer, undefeated in twenty-six bouts, and he'd sparred with the best of them—Willie Pep, Barney Ross, Solly Krieger, even Kid Gavilan and 'Sugar Ray' Robinson—and he was an amazing storehouse of anecdotes and facts, especially about Jewish fighters. He could name them all—Ross, Leonard, Tendler, Attell, 'Battling' Levinsky, 'Slapsie Maxie' Rosenbloom, Lesnevich, and he loved to be able to point out, when people brought up Baer as the greatest of them all (Baer had killed two men in fights, including Frankie Campbell, the brother of the Brooklyn Dodgers' first baseman, 'Dolph' Camilli), that even though Baer wore a Star of David on his trunks, he was less of a Jew than Jack Dempsey. Baer's paternal grandfather, a butcher, was *probably* Jewish, Herschel would say, but Dempsey's maternal grandmother, Rachel Solomon, was *truly* Jewish, and that made Dempsey a Jew in his book, and surely would have made him a Jew if he'd been living in Hitler's Germany.

What also surprised me was that most of the men, Louis included, had great respect for Max Schmeling, who'd been known as 'Hitler's boxer,' and who'd beaten Louis for the world championship in their first fight, then lost to him in the first round of their famous rematch, but who, according to Herschel, had been 'a real *mensch*' to Louis, and—Louis nodded agreement— was now helping him out financially in his battles with thugs from the Internal Revenue Service.

On our second day in Lakewood, Joey took me on a drive around the area—a first—just the two of us, and when we drove past a house that was up a long driveway, partway into the woods—a colonial style building that looked as if it had once been a classy hotel, but which clearly, starting with rusted cars in the front yard, had fallen on hard times—he told me that this was probably the house he was born in: one of the places where the women my mother helped out lived while they waited for their children to be born.

The house is surely gone by now, and that part of the world's been taken over by Jews, not only Chassidic Jews with their huge families, but modern Orthodox Jews, and middle-class Jews who prefer to own their own homes or condos near New York City rather than retire to assisted living places in Florida. Years later, when Joey was drinking hard and deep in the soup one night, I asked him about the house, and about the women who lived in them—asked if he'd ever wanted to find out who his mother was—and he got a sudden wild-fire in his eyes, as if, had he been sober, he would have tried to kill me, and he said that say what you would, the women in those places were all sluts.

"Oh come on—!" I began, but he grabbed me by the front of my shirt. "Yeah, yeah—I know all about it," he said, cutting me off, "the way you people think now—how the guys were dishonorable shits and didn't pay the price women did—but say what you will, they were all dirty sluts, my mother included."

I was stunned by the venom in his voice, but when we were driving around the Lakewood area together that first time, I loved him so much I would never have dreamt he could have had such a vicious, unkind thought in his head. That was also the day he explained how it all worked: how when families of pregnant young women came to certain doctors—after they found out their lousy news and wanted to avoid the shame that would accompany an illegitimate birth—these doctors would tell them there was an alternative to the danger of abortion, and refer them to doctors like Margolies who were associated with lawyers who could guarantee that the women we now call 'birth-mothers' would never know to which families their infants were given away. The lawyers also took care of whatever papers were needed—health forms, birth certificates—and dealt with financial arrangements, and with people in the Lakewood area who needed to be paid off for looking the other way. For this, Joey said, his father's connections with gambling big shots, many of whom vacationed in the Lakewood area and spent time at training camps like the one I went to with Joey and Herschel, had been helpful. He also said that no matter what my mother said about him, he never took offense because in his eyes she'd always be the most courageous woman he knew—that it was because of women like her that guys like him got a break in life.

On our third and last day at the camp, Herschel taped up

my hands, brought me headgear and gloves, and put me in the ring with a young professional fighter named Danny Mancuso, who was about my weight, maybe one-forty, and bet that even though I'd never been in a ring before, given how good an athlete I was, I could go three rounds with Mancuso without being knocked down. I looked to Joey, who gave me a big grin and said he was going to lay a hundred smackers on me against any and all takers.

Herschel took me aside, coached me on some basics—jab, jab, slip, slip—how, after I jabbed, to move my head quickly to the side to avoid a return blow—and said that the main thing was not the hands, but the legs. "Balance, Marty," he said. "Make sure you got good balance, especially when you move from side to side—and when you see an opening and swing, maintain your balance—don't let your back leg drag, got it?"

I said I did, but when the bell rang and I stepped into the ring, my legs turned to jelly, and as Mancuso danced around and threw jabs—I was able to catch most of them with my gloves—and then laughed at me for being a pretty boy whose nose he'd try not to break, my stomach gurgled so loud I thought everyone would hear it.

Between rounds, Herschel told me I'd done a good job of keeping away from Mancuso's right hand, which he said was wicked. "He's just playing with you," Herschel said, "and he got no clue that you're gonna surprise him."

"I am?" I said.

"Oh yeah," Herschel said, "because he's got the same problem Louis had with Schmeling in their first fight. When he goes for the knockout punch—a roundhouse right—he drops his left hand, which leaves him wide open. That's when you're in the money."

My legs were better in the second round, and I enjoyed moving around the ring, and listening to Joey, Herschel, and some of the others cheering for me, and once in a while jabbing at

Mancuso and connecting, then getting him in a clinch so I could catch my breath. What surprised me, though, was how *tired* my arms got just from keeping them up all the time to protect myself.

"This is it, Marty," Joey called when the bell rang for the third round. "So don't forget—my money's on you, and that there's nothing I hate more than losing."

About a minute into the round I heard Mancuso's trainer yelling at him to stop fooling around and put me on my ass or they'd lose whatever bucks they'd put down against Joey. Mancuso came after me then, and I got up on the balls of my feet more, my knees slightly bent—as if I were guarding a guy who was trying to fake me out and make his move to the basket—and when he came at me with a couple of sharp jabs to soften me up, and I could tell he was going to unleash his right, I was ready, and just before he threw his right, he dropped his left the way Herschel said he would, and I laid into his stomach as hard as I could—as close to where Herschel had shown me the liver was, the most vulnerable spot on the body—and when Mancuso gagged and doubled over, I smashed him with a wild punch to the side of his head with all my might, then stepped away and, to my amazement, watched him fall flat onto the canvas.

Joey and Herschel howled with delight—roared out my name—and Mancuso stumbled to his feet, came at me again, but was too wobbly to land any good punches, and at the end of the round, Joey climbed into the ring, held my right hand high in triumph, and then walked around, his hand moving in and out between the ropes, to collect the money he'd won. "Come on, come on, guys," he kept saying. "Pay up! Pay up!"

That night, after Joey passed out and two guys helped him back to our cabin, Herschel told me he was worried about Joey. "He saw a lot of shit when he was overseas," Herschel said, "and he won't talk to nobody about it—just sucks it all in, and then drowns it in booze. So you keep an eye on him too, okay?"

I said I would, but what could I do, really? The more money he made, the more he drank, and having a loving wife and two gorgeous kids and everything money could buy didn't seem to make a difference. Sometimes, when I was home from college (I went to Union, a small upstate New York college where I was able to start on the basketball team by my junior year), and I stopped by his office, he'd take a bottle of Scotch and some paper cups from the bottom drawer in his desk and offer me a drink, and when I'd say no thanks, he'd tell me how smart I was, smarter than he'd ever be, and ask me what I thought he should do because he knew if he kept drinking the way he was, he'd wind up losing everything.

I said ordinary stuff—that he should talk to his doctor, or maybe go to one of the places movie stars and athletes went when they had to chill out—and he'd say that what I said made sense, and that he was going to think it over, and then he'd pour himself another drink.

My senior year in college, his business went into the tank. What happened was that after a big Davy Crockett craze, with pretty much every kid in the country wearing a coonskin hat, he'd bet on there being a big Robin Hood craze next, but wound up with two warehouses full of Robin Hood stuff nobody wanted. He went bankrupt, drank more, and—no surprise to anyone, including my parents and Herschel—Carol divorced him. But within eighteen months or so, with money Herschel put together from people he knew, Joey was back in business, and, specializing in sportswear for golf and tennis—shirts, shorts, pants, caps—his business boomed again, and when I saw him the summer after I graduated from Union, he told me he was on top of the world, and—he whispered this—he thanked me for the advice I'd given him, and said that when he told everybody he was voting himself a Carribean cruise so he could put his feet up and meet some elegant ladies, he'd been in a detox center in Arizona.

When his business failed a second time, though, he went back on the bottle big-time, and this happened during a year when I was teaching at a prep school in New Jersey, which was also the year I fell in love, really in love, for the first time. Until then, in college and during my first year after college, I'd had some girl-friends, but nothing serious, and had mostly been doing what Joey believed I should be doing: trying to become a writer. I'd received encouragement from some of my professors, and had passed the substitute license test for New York City teachers, so that I could earn enough to pay my keep, and, on the days I didn't get a call to sub, have my time free for writing.

I rented a one-room walk-up apartment on the top floor of a brownstone in the West Eighties—this was in 1963—and I paid my landlord, a mannerly Hungarian man named Mordecai Wenger, fifteen dollars a week for the room. I shared two bath-rooms with three other residents of the floor, and once a week Mister Wenger would come by, clean the room, and change my linens. And whenever I saw Joey, which was about once every other week, no matter how broke or drunk he was, when we parted, he'd always put a fifty dollar bill in my hand, chuck me on the shoulder, tell me how terrific he thought it was that I was going to be a writer, and to remember what Jack Dempsey said—that he'd been a pretty good fighter, but that it was the *writers* who'd made him great.

I finished a draft of a novel that year—a story about an up-and-coming young boxer who interrupts his boxing career to enlist in the army, and who winds up—where else?—in the Far East, nearly dies fighting the Japanese on Guadalcanal, and who comes home, gets married, has two kids, and has to give up his dream—to become World Middleweight Champion—partly be-cause of responsibilities to his family, but more because there are lots of new, fit, young fighters against whom, with his war wounds and his age, he's now easy prey. I did most of my re-search for the book by reading every writer I could find who'd written a war novel—Mailer, Jones, Shaw, Cozzens, Wouk, Michener, Uris, Hersey—and I had purposely *not* given my hero a drinking problem in case the book was published and Joey and people who knew him read it.

Although a few editors found the book "promising," and asked to see my *next* novel, I was easily discouraged by rejection, stopped writing, and took the first job I applied for: teaching English at a fancy prep school in New Jersey, near Saddle River.

Doctor Margaret Whitmore—Margaret *Connolly* Whitmore—she'd emphasize, as a way of showing that although she might *appear* to have come from an old-line WASP family, she had good Irish blood in her too—was head of the school's English Department. She was going on forty, about fifteen years older than I was, was drop-dead beautiful in the cool way movie stars like Grace Kelly and Dina Merrill were, and had a reputation for being so no-nonsense with faculty and students that she was known, behind her back, as 'Doctor Iceberg.' When I asked other teachers about her, they all said the same thing—that she was brilliant, ran a tight ship, did not suffer fools gladly, and that her private life was a total mystery.

I kept my distance, did a serviceable job with my classes—I found that I enjoyed reading and talking about novels and stories much more than I enjoyed *writing* them—and so I was surprised one day in the teacher's lunchroom, when she sat down next to me.

"I've noticed that you've grown thinner since the start of the semester, and that you provide yourself with quite meagre provisions," she said, setting a plate of food in front of me. "I cook most evenings, and it's just as easy to cook for two as for one. I hope you'll like what I made."

She was so direct in the way she talked that I hesitated even to say thank you. But I did, and for the next ten days or so, she'd sit next to me at lunch each day, and put a plate of food in front of me: lamb and beef stews, exotic chicken dishes, sandwiches with sautéed vegetables, cheeses, and herbs. If there were raised eyebrows among the faculty, I was unaware of them, and that was probably because she set my plate down in the same matter-of-fact way she did everything else, after which she'd turn to others and engage them in conversation, or simply stare ahead in the confident way she had, so that no one dared to even *try* to open a conversation with her.

Then one afternoon, in the parking lot after school, she stopped me and said that since I seemed fond of her cooking, perhaps, if I was not otherwise engaged, I would enjoy having dinner with her at her home the following evening.

I said yes.

My first thought, given her age, was that I might find a way to introduce her to Joey, and that maybe she'd turn out to be the kind of woman who, when it came to men, was into rescue work, and would see Joey as a reclamation project. And maybe, too, their outer differences—her elegance, his street-savvy roughness—masked inner similarities: an elegant sensitivity in him, a rough, raw passion in her—that would prove a winning combination.

At dinner the next evening, when she asked me to tell her about myself—things beyond what she knew from my application and interview—I found myself talking about growing up in Brooklyn, and about Joey: about the ups and downs of his life—how he'd been a war hero, a great ballplayer, and had been adopted as a black market baby. I couldn't *stop* talking about him, and, helped along by a smooth red wine she kept refilling my glass with, in an easy way I'd never talked with anyone *other* than Joey.

Margaret lived in a two-story Victorian house that had gleaming parquet floors, stained glass windows, and pocket doors separating the downstairs rooms—living room, dining room, kitchen—from one another. It was furnished with antiques of a kind I remembered seeing in the lounges of fancy women's

167

colleges I'd been to, and after we finished eating and were sitting across from each other in her living room, drinking more wine—she'd closed the pocket doors—she said she was intrigued by my mention of black market babies—that our conversation made her recall that she had heard the term several times when she was growing up in Philadelphia, and she wondered if I would be willing to tell her a bit more about them. She would understand, of course, if I'd rather not, but when she smiled at me warmly—a different smile from any I'd ever seen from her before—I began talking not only about Joey, and what I knew about how Herschel and Rose got him, but about Lakewood, and about my mother and Doctor Margolies.

I kept talking and drinking, drinking and talking, and at one point I must have fallen asleep because when I looked up, she was standing above me, as serenely calm as ever, and saying, as if she were responding to something I'd just said, that yes, my mother must have been an exceptional woman, though doubtless difficult at times, and she wondered how she was doing.

I said my mother had died of breast cancer four months before the start of the school year, and that my father had died ten months before that—they were only in their early fifties, both of them—which events, I suggested, made me an orphan, didn't they?

"In which case," she said, "although you did not murder them, you may still throw yourself on the mercy of the court, yes?"

"That's an old one," I said. "The definition of *chutzpah*, right? And I'm an English teacher, so I should know my definitions, right?"

I tried to stand, started to fall, but instead of catching me, she touched my shoulder lightly with a single finger so that I fell straight back into the armchair I'd been asleep in.

"Clearly, you cannot drive home tonight," she said, "so I will prepare the guest room for you."

She did, and the next thing I knew I heard a knock on the door, and she was looking in and telling me I should shower and shave, and then come downstairs for breakfast.

When I had dinner at Margaret's house the following evening, she said that one reason among many that allowed her to be quite optimistic about the future of our friendship was that I had not apologized for what had happened the previous night.

"What happened last night?" I asked.

"Exactly," she said.

We had dinner together every school night for the next two weeks, and we talked about all kinds of things—not so much about our childhoods (she'd grown up one of three daughters of a wealthy high-line Philadelphia family that had made its fortune in coal by-products, coke especially, had gone to Bryn Mawr, and then to the University of Pennsylvania for her doctorate in English), but more about our daily lives: students in the school we especially liked or were worried about; other teachers and their quirks; and, most of all, about books. She had done her dissertation on the novels of Thomas Hardy, and we found particular delight in the discovery that we both considered the first hundred pages or so of *The Mayor of Casterbridge* to be the most perfect opening of any novel either of us had ever read.

We talked about authors we loved—Dickens, James, Cather, Dos Passos, Flaubert—and she introduced me to authors I'd known about but never read, and came to love: Robert Louis Stevenson, Arnold Bennett, George Eliot, and two modern writers especially dear to her: Colette and Jean Rhys. She assumed I wanted to be a writer—doesn't every child who grows up loving to read dream of becoming a writer one day? she said—and when I told her I'd already written a novel, but, discouraged by the rejections it received, was reluctant to start another, she asked if she might read it. A week later, on the evening before

I'd made a date for us to drive into New York City to have dinner with Joey, I gave her the manuscript.

The three of us met at Da Nico, an Italian restaurant on Mulberry Street, where, Joey told us, his father had known the original owner, and where, when he was a kid, he and his father would go whenever they had something special to celebrate. And what were the usual occasions for celebration? Margaret asked.

"Winning," Joey said. "My father and I were big on winning."

"Winning what?" Margaret said.

"You name it," Joey said. "Ballgames, horse races, fights, wars…" He looked away for a split-second, and then put on his great smile—his *winning* smile, I thought to myself—and told Margaret the story of how he and his father had made seven hundred bucks betting on me when I'd knocked down a good young professional fighter in Lakewood.

Joey looked trim and healthy, as if he'd been on the wagon for a while—and he was as charming as a guy could be, telling Margaret he'd heard a lot about her—about how brilliant she was, and how she'd taken me under her wing, and that for his money there was nobody who did better under a good wing than I did.

He asked her lots of questions about herself, and she answered them without the clipped coldness I was used to from school, and seemed to be flirting with him from time to time with easy banter about the shirt business, and what the rules were about giving someone the shirt off your back. Early in the evening, she even suggested he might enjoy taking a drive out to the country some weekend, so he could see our school, which was built on what had once been an estate owned by heirs to the Singer Sewing Machine fortune, and when she said this, I said that if he did, I bet we might persuade her to make one of her incredible gourmet meals for us, and told the story of how she'd begun bringing me lunch, and how we'd been having dinners together regularly.

About midway through the meal, when she went to the ladies room, Joey whacked me on the shoulder, and congratulated me.

"For what?"

"For getting your ashes hauled regularly by one very classy lady," he said.

"But—" I began.

"And she is one classy piece of prime ass, Marty, because in my experience, see, the ones who are cold bitches on the outside got the most heat going on the inside." He lifted his glass of wine in a toast to me. "More power to your elbow, buddy—and to its southern neighbor."

Joey finished his wine, and ordered a Scotch-on-the-rocks. I thought of telling him that things weren't like that—that Margaret and I weren't sleeping together, that we were just friends— but I was afraid that if I did he would have looked down on me in the way my mother used to look down on my father.

So I said nothing—just grinned back at him as if to corroborate what he thought was going on—and when Margaret returned, and asked him about *his* life, saying she'd heard he'd left the garment business for a new enterprise, Joey tossed down his Scotch, and ordered another. Given that the garment business was heading South and overseas at full speed, he explained, what he was doing while he figured out his next move was calling in favors from old friends for part-time jobs at resorts in the Lakewood area and the Catskills, usually as a maitre d', but not, given his checkered history, as a bartender, which was a shame, because that was where the good money at those places was.

By the time our coffee came, his voice slurred, Joey was going on and on about how much he missed his wife and kids (he only saw his son and daughter one afternoon a month), how nobody would ever know what his father had gone through to help him out when he'd gotten into bad trouble with some wise guys, and about his war buddies and how he missed them, the ones who were still living as much as the ones who weren't.

When he apologized for his drinking—"I'm too much of a slob to be associating with classy dudes like you two," he said—Margaret responded by saying that she trusted we would see one another again soon, and that, in her experience, it was hardly tragic when a celebratory event—our dinner and meeting—became more celebratory than anticipated. The best moments in life, she said, as in good novels—and when she said this, she reached over—a first—and held my hand briefly—are those that are unpredictable.

"That wins for me!" Joey exclaimed, and we all laughed.

At dinner the next evening, Margaret said that she had, of course, been thinking about Joey a good deal, and about my relationship with him. Having met him, and understanding why, as a boy, I would have looked up to him the way I did, had reinforced a wish she had for the two of us.

"I think he was quite shrewd when he said what he did about you doing well when kept under a good wing," she said.

I shrugged. "So—?"

She stood and walked around the table to me, touched my face gently. "I've decided to take you under *my* wing," she said, "and I hope you'll consent."

Even though, despite the arch way she put it, I understood immediately what she was talking about—I hadn't been without my own fantasies—I still gasped to hear the words come from her mouth.

"So?" she asked. "What do you say?"

"Thank you?" I replied.

"*Thank you?!*" she laughed. Then she kissed me. I kissed her back, stood, pressed her to me, and when I started to probe her lips with my tongue, she stepped back.

"Be patient, Marty," she said. "It's the main thing. We'll do much better—we'll be capable of more unique pleasures, and of the often sublime understandings that accompany pleasure—when we learn to be patient."

What she told me later that night, when we lay next to each other in her bed, was that the quality that drew her to me was my combination of innocence and enthusiasm. What I clearly lacked, and what she believed she was capable of providing—think William Blake, she said—was experience. I had a rare sensibility for a young man of my background, and what excited her were the ways in which she might nurture it. She had been waiting for a young man like me for many years, felt fortunate to have found me, and hoped she would be able to help me learn about the many good and beautiful things of life: books, of course, and food, and wines, and music, and sex.

I was too happy—enthralled, enchanted—to object strenuously, though I did protest mildly, saying that even though she was somewhat older, and held a higher position at our school, I wasn't thrilled with the idea of us being in a student-teacher relationship.

"That is not the right way to think about it," she said and, telling me that I was not to move, no matter what impulses arose in me, she began, very slowly, to make love to me again.

In the evenings, and on weekends, she started introducing me to wines—how to taste and evaluate them—and to music I was unfamiliar with (she would, for example, play two recordings of a movement from a Bartok or Dvorak string quartet, and we'd discuss their differences)—and on some evenings we would take turns reading passages from novels to one another, then talking about what it was in what we'd read that seemed especially unusual, remarkable, or wanting.

We never drove to or from school together, and on weekends we did not frequent local restaurants or movie theaters. Instead, we either stayed home, sometimes, except for going downstairs to get food, remaining in bed together for an entire twenty-four hours, or we drove into the city and went to museums, concerts, and the theater. In public, we never touched, and though this frustrated me no end—I wanted, always always, to be touching her, holding her hand, having her fingers touching my arm or neck—she seemed to have no difficulty in keeping a discreet distance, nor was she flattered or amused when I told her how frustrating the situation was for me. Discretion, she declared once, was not only the better part of valor, but central to what Flaubert thought of as a true sentimental education—meaning not an education that was *emotionally* sentimental, and therefore shallow, but an education in the sentiments themselves.

On a Sunday evening, five weeks after I'd begun living with her, she told me that she had finished reading my novel.

"What I think," she said—we'd finished dinner, but were still at the dining room table—"is that despite its many merits— you certainly have a good ear and a good heart, and there are some quite vivid, affecting scenes—the publishers have probably done you a favor by not publishing this book."

I was devastated—felt tears rush to my eyes—but controlled myself and looked straight at her. "And—?" I asked.

"And what?"

"What else?"

"There's nothing more to say, really," she said. "Except—"

"Except *what*?" I asked.

"I trust you'll take what I say next as kindness—something I say to you as your friend, though I am sure it may not feel that way to you at first," she said. "Although you have some gifts, and surely do not lack for fortitude—your Brooklyn roots have given you the ability to compete, to stay the course, and to want, like your cousin, to win at anything you do, I believe your *desire* to be a writer is—how best to put it, and in language you will understand—?"

"Just say it, for Christ's sake," I demanded.

She looked at me with a half-smile but didn't speak.

"Patience, right?" I said. "Patience. Sure."

"I think, given what I know about you, that your desire to be a writer, inspired by your cousin during your impressionable years, is a bit like the ambition a young baseball fan might have for becoming a professional player some day," she said. "It is quite understandable, and, as with many excellent athletes, there are often viable reasons to encourage certain youngsters. Still, in my judgment, which is surely fallible, you were made for other things—better things, things more consonant with—"

"Fuck you," I said, and left the room.

I drove back to my apartment in Ridgefield that night, and stayed away from her house until the next weekend. At school, we passed each other in the hallways the way we always had, with no acknowledgement that anything out of the ordinary had occurred. I brought my lunch with me—sandwiches and fruit—and ate outside, in the gardens near the baseball field, so that I didn't have to see her in the lunchroom.

By Saturday, though, I couldn't take it anymore, and I drove out to her house. Her car was in the driveway, but when I knocked on the door she didn't answer it. I opened the door, walked through the downstairs rooms, then went upstairs.

She was sitting in a chair, looking out a window at the backyard, and did not turn toward me.

I touched her shoulder, bent down to kiss her, but she lowered her head to her chest.

"I missed you," I said, "and I'm sorry I left the way I did."

She looked up at me then, and I was shocked: she seemed to have aged twenty years since I'd seen her in school the day before. Her face was ashen, her eyes red and swollen, her voice, when she spoke, without affect.

"I hurt you badly but I couldn't help myself," she said, looking down again and playing with a set of keys on her lap.

"Are you *okay*?" I asked.

She shrugged.

"Can you talk to me—can you say anything?"

"What's there to say?" she said, but without looking at me, after which, despite my asking her a bunch more questions, she did nothing but stare at her lap.

"Are you sick—should I call a doctor?" I asked after a while.

She shrugged again. "I didn't want you to see me this way," she said.

"*Which* way?"

"It's an old story, and for the most part we are successful at keeping most of the demons at bay most of the time…"

"What are you talking about?" I asked, and brought a chair over, sat and faced her. "*What* demons—?"

"Mine," she said, without smiling.

"But I *love* you," I said. "I want to know what happened—what's wrong—what's going on—"

"You're quite sweet," she said, "and you have nothing to do with this. Nobody does. I shouldn't be here, really."

"Then where should you be?"

"Nowhere."

I kept at it for a while, trying to get a response from her—any response—but nothing I said made a difference. I *was* able to get her to walk downstairs with me to the kitchen, but she wouldn't let me touch her, much less kiss her or hold her, and though she did drink a glass of water I brought for her, she refused all other food and drink.

I stayed for an hour or two, and when I returned the next day, she and her car were gone. At school on Monday, when I stopped by her office after my first class, she greeted me in the brisk, impersonal way she greeted everybody. She looked the way she usually did—beautiful, poised, clear-eyed, with nothing in her appearance or manner that suggested she had ever been the woman I'd been with two mornings before, or during all the weeks that had preceded that morning.

When, three weeks later, on a Thursday evening, I received a call from Herschel telling me that Joey was gone, and that the funeral would take place in Brooklyn the next morning—they'd found him dead in a motel room in the Catskills of an apparent heart attack—and when I telephoned Margaret to say that

I would not be in school the next day, and why, she offered me condolences on my loss, said she was glad she had been able to meet a man who had played such a significant role in my life, and that if I needed to stay away from school past the coming Monday, I should let her know and she would arrange matters.

"I really loved him," I said, and started to cry. "I really did…"

"I know," she said. "Early, unexpected losses are the most difficult of all, aren't they?"

It turned out that when Joey died, he wasn't working as a maitre d', but had been going from motel to motel in the Catskills, and along the Jersey shore and in the Lakewood area, selling machines that attached to beds and into which you put quarters that made the mattresses vibrate and gave you what were advertised as 'magic-finger massages.'

Neither Herschel nor Rose ever mentioned Joey's name again. Rose died ten months later, and Herschel became a recluse, staying in his Upper West Side Manhattan apartment and emerging only to get food, and, once in a while, when I was in town, to go to the fights, either at Madison Square Garden or the old Saint Nick's Arena on West 66th Street.

I left the prep school at the end of the year, enrolled in the graduate English program at the State University of New York at Stony Brook, got a Ph.D. in English with a dissertation on the novels of Robert Louis Stevenson, and became a professor of English at Hamilton College, in Clinton, New York, a good small liberal arts school similar to Union College. Helene Maubert, an English teacher in a Clinton high school, in order to to gain credits toward a master's degree, enrolled in a course I was teaching—'The Modern Novel'—and we were married nine months later, in Rensselaerville, a small town south of Albany where she'd grown up. We lived in Clinton for the next three decades, raised our daughters there, and it was only after Helene's death and my retirement from teaching that, at my daughter's urgings, I moved back to New York City. I never revised my first novel or wrote another one. I became Chair of the Hamilton College English Department though, and contented myself with building an excellent department and, in my teaching—introductory literature courses especially—with trying to impart a love of reading to several generations of students.

In New York, I bought an apartment on the Upper West Side, a few blocks from where Carolyn and her family were living, and not far from Herschel, and was able, until his death seven months ago, to get him to leave his apartment and have breakfast with me on a regular basis, Tuesdays and Thursday mornings, at a local diner, where we would read through the sports pages together, and I'd tell him about my children and grandchildren. On occasion, I'd try to get him to talk about Joey by remarking on the golden olden days and how things had changed—how, for example—my most pointed attempt to draw him out—in earlier times people looking to adopt children wanted only healthy, white babies, but how, with some parallels to the changing ethnicities of boxing champions, which reflected changing patterns of immigration, people had come to accept the adopting of black, Hispanic, and Asian children as normal. Nothing I said could get him to talk about Joey, however, or about what life was like for us before Joey died.

I suspected, of course, that the story of Joey's motel heart attack was a cover-up, but there was no way to find out the truth without pressing Herschel, and hurting him, and what difference would it make if I found out that Joey had done himself in? All that mattered was that he was gone, and much too soon. The same went for Margaret. I received regular alumni magazines and newsletters from our school, and knew that, three years after I left, she had resigned her position there. For a few years after that, I'd ask some of the teachers I kept in touch with if they knew anything about what she was doing, and after Helene died I even 'Googled' her name several times to see if I could find out about her, and, perhaps, I thought, be in touch. But my searches all led to dead ends, as, too literally, did other matters.

Three months after Herschel's death, I received a call from Carolyn, asking me to please hurry and meet her at Roosevelt Hospital, in the Intensive Care Unit. Something had happened to Amos.

What had happened was that he had developed what seemed at first an ordinary rash—red spots accompanied by dark dots, and by several mysterious marks that looked like bruises even though there were no apparent causes for any bruising. By the time I arrived at the hospital, he had slipped into a coma, and though the doctors were doing all they could, they were not optimistic.

Amos died that night of what was diagnosed as a form of toxic meningitis—meningococcemia was the technical term for a bacterial infection that could take the lives of children, when they contracted it, within twenty-four hours. The doctors had given Amos massive doses of antibiotics, but by the time treatment began, it was already too late. There was an effective vaccine against the disease, I later learned, but the vaccine, except in rare instances, was given only to adolescents.

Amos was, it occurred to me when, at the cemetery, we lowered his casket into the ground, about the age I was when Joey had come home from the war. We sat *shiva* for Amos in the traditional way we'd sat *shiva* for Joey (and for Rose, and for my parents, and for all my parents' brothers and sisters), and during the seven days of mourning I found myself staying close to my granddaughter Deborah, Amos's sister, as if believing my presence could in some way be protective, even though I knew it couldn't—that in this life there was mostly pain and loss and worry, with now and then a whiff of hope or pleasure, and that if you thought you heard the flutter of wings, as I recalled Joey telling me once—something he brought back from his time overseas—chances were even-money you'd been cold-cocked and that the best thing to do was to pray the flutter you heard was coming from one of your guardian angels and not the angel of death.

When we were together that week, I found myself thinking about Joey more than I had in many years, and when I thought about him, I thought mostly about the day he showed me the house in which he thought he might have been born, and of the easy way he and Joe Louis had with each other, and of the fact that Louis, our greatest heavyweight champion—one hundred forty consecutive months of taking on and defeating all comers—had not, according to those who knew him, spoken a word until he was about six, the age Amos had been. Like his mother, who'd died in a lunatic asylum, Louis also spent time—this was near the end of his life when he was broke and addicted to drugs—in a psychiatric hospital, and when he passed away in 1981, at sixty-six, and I'd told Herschel I was pleased to hear that Schmeling had helped pay for Louis's funeral, Herschel laughed at me. Given that Louis was buried at Arlington National Cemetery, he said, it was our taxes that paid for his funeral.

And Schmeling? Schmeling—a man who would wind up dying seven months short of his one hundredth birthday, outliving not only Louis and Herschel, but virtually everyone who'd ever known him—Schmeling had probably come to believe he'd paid for Louis's funeral since he'd come to believe pretty much every other distortion and lie written about him. This was a gift of character Louis lacked, Herschel said, and he added that looking back he'd come to see that Schmeling was nothing more than an out-and-out opportunist, a man who'd devoted his life to staying fit, and to pleasing anyone and everyone, including the Nazis. But when we were together the week of Amos's death, which had followed so soon after Herschel's, and in visits afterward, I didn't talk about this, or say the obvious to Carolyn or Carl, or to Michelle and her husband Phil—that, beyond the age of childbearing, Carolyn and Carl were now out of spares.

Also published by TWO DOLLAR RADIO

ALSO BY JAY NEUGEBOREN

1940
A NOVEL

A Trade Paperback Original; 978-0-9763895-6-9; $15.00 US

* Long list, 2010 International IMPAC Dublin
  Literary Award.

"Jay Neugeboren traverses the Hitlerian tightrope with all the skill and formal daring that have made him one of our most honored writers of literary fiction and masterful nonfiction."
—Tim Rutten, *Los Angeles Times*

SET ON THE eve of America's entry into World War Two, *1940* is built around a fascinating historical figure, Dr. Eduard Bloch, an Austrian doctor who had been physician to Adolf Hitler and his familiy when Hitler was a boy. The historical Bloch was the only Jew for whom Hitler ever personally arranged departure from Europe, and he must now, living in the Bronx, face accusations over the special treatment he received.

1940 FOCUSES ON Dr. Bloch's relationship with Elizabeth Rofman, a medical illustrator at Johns Hopkins Medical School, who has come to New York from Baltimore to visit her father, only to find that he has mysteriously disappeared. The story grows more complex when Elizabeth's son Daniel, a disturbed young adolescent, escapes from the institution in Maryland where his parents have committed him, and makes his way to New York, where he is hidden and protected by his mother... and by Dr. Bloch.

THE VISITING SUIT
A NOVEL BY XIAODA XIAO

A Trade Paperback Original; 978-0-9820151-7-9; $16.50 US

"[Xiao] recount[s] his struggle in sometimes unexpectedly lovely detail. Against great odds, in the grimmest of settings, he manages to find good in the darkness."
—Lori Soderlind, *New York Times Book Review*

THE CAVE MAN
A NOVEL BY XIAODA XIAO

A Trade Paperback Original; 978-0-9820151-3-1; $15.50 US

* *WOSU* (an NPR member station) Favorite Book of 2009.

"As a parable of modern China, [*The Cave Man*] is chilling."
—*Boston Globe*

THE ORANGE EATS CREEPS
A NOVEL BY GRACE KRILANOVICH
A Trade Paperback Original; 978-0-9820151-8-6; $16 US
* National Book Foundation 2010 '5 Under 35' Selection.
* *NPR* Best Books of 2010.

"Krilanovich's work will make you believe that new ways of storytelling are still emerging from the margins." —*NPR*

TERMITE PARADE
A NOVEL BY JOSHUA MOHR
A Trade Paperback Original; 978-0-9820151-6-2; $16.00 US
* *Sacramento Bee* Best Read of 2010.

"[A] wry and unnerving story of bad love gone rotten. [Mohr] has a generous understanding of his characters, whom he describes with an intelligence and sensitivity that pulls you in. This is no small achievement." —*New York Times Book Review*

SOME THINGS THAT MEANT THE WORLD TO ME
A NOVEL BY JOSHUA MOHR
A Trade Paperback Original; 978-0-9820151-1-7; $15.50 US
* *O, The Oprah Magazine* '10 Terrific Reads of 2009.'

"Charles Bukowski fans will dig the grit in this seedy novel, a poetic rendering of postmodern San Francisco."
—*O, The Oprah Magazine*

THE PEOPLE WHO WATCHED HER PASS BY
A NOVEL BY SCOTT BRADFIELD
A Trade Paperback Original; 978-0-9820151-5-5; $14.50 US

"Challenging [and] original… A billowy adventure of a book. In a book that supplies few answers, Bradfield's lavish eloquence is the presiding constant."
—*New York Times Book Review*